Christmas Miracles in Maternity

Hope, magic and precious new beginnings at Teddy's!

Welcome to Teddy's Centre for Babies and Birth, where the brightest stars of neonatal and obstetric medicine work tirelessly to save tiny lives and deliver bundles of joy all year round—but there's never a time quite as magical as Christmas!

Although the temperature might be dropping outside, unexpected surprises are heating up for these dedicated pros! And as Christmas Day draws near, secrets are revealed, hope is ignited and love takes over.

Cuddle up this Christmas with the heartwarming stories of the doctors, nurses, midwives and surgeons at Teddy's in the **Christmas Miracles in Maternity** miniseries:

The Nurse's Christmas Gift
by Tina Beckett

The Midwife's Pregnancy Miracle
by Kate Hardy

White Christmas for the Single Mom
by Susanne Hampton

A Royal Baby for Christmas
by Scarlet Wilson

All available now!

Dear Reader,

In this Christmas story, my heroine, Dr. Juliet Turner, is transferred from a hot Australian summer to the snow-covered Cotswolds. Ordinarily this wouldn't be an issue for her, a young, single, world-renowned specialist, but while Juliet has no man to hold her back, she *does* have a four-year-old daughter, Bea, to consider. Despite her reservations, it appears that Juliet is the only one concerned about her taking Bea on this adventure that will include their first white Christmas alone on the other side of the world.

But *will* it be a Christmas alone? Pretty quickly Bea thinks that her mother's nemesis, handsome ob-gyn Dr. Charlie Warren, might just be a suitable daddy. Although widower Charlie finds moments of joy with the little girl and her mother, he is still burdened with overwhelming guilt over his wife's death. Can Charlie step from behind the cloud that darkens his life? And can Juliet learn to trust again after being left after only one night with Bea's biological father? Love has healing properties like nothing else, and that is just what Charlie and Juliet need to leave their pain behind. Will a white Christmas bring this single mom the happiness she deserves?

I hope you enjoy Juliet and Charlie's journey to happily-ever-after, and I wish you all a very Merry Christmas filled with love!

Warmest regards,

Susanne

WHITE CHRISTMAS FOR THE SINGLE MOM

———

SUSANNE HAMPTON

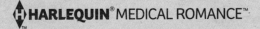

Special thanks and acknowledgment are given to Susanne Hampton for her contribution to the Christmas Miracles in Maternity series.

Recycling programs for this product may not exist in your area.

ISBN-13: 978-0-373-01161-2

White Christmas for the Single Mom

First North American Publication 2016

Copyright © 2016 by Harlequin Books S.A.

This edition published by arrangement with Harlequin Books S.A.

For questions and comments about the quality of this book, please contact us at CustomerService@Harlequin.com.

Printed in U.S.A.

Thank you to the wonderfully talented and incredibly witty Harlequin authors who shared this writing journey with me…Scarlet Wilson, Kate Hardy and Tina Beckett. You have made writing this book like a road trip with new friends. You all helped to make it a joyful experience and one I will never forget.

And to my amazing editor, Nicola…thank you again for your guidance and unending patience as we brought this book to life.

Praise for
Susanne Hampton

"A stunning read about new beginnings that is guaranteed to melt any reader's heart."
—*Goodreads* on
Falling for Dr. December

"Probably one of my top ten favorite reads this year. It was heartbreaking…kept me wanting to read to find out what happens next."
—*Goodreads* on
A Baby to Bind Them

CHAPTER ONE

IT WAS FOUR in the morning and snow was gently falling in the darkness like tiny stars floating to the ground when Charlie Warren awoke from a nightmare that was all too familiar. Beads of perspiration trailed over his half-naked body. The nights it happened were less in number than the year before but they still came with a regularity he found strangely comforting. Feeling the pain was better than feeling nothing. Or facing the fear of letting go completely. That was something he could still not bring himself to contemplate.

For the few hours that sleep claimed him during those nights, Charlie would relive the moments of impact. Sounds echoed in his mind, each as haunting as the one before. The buckling metal and splintering glass as his car skidded out of his control and slammed into the old oak tree. It was the crash that had claimed his wife and had come close to claiming Charlie's sanity. He would wake and in the deafening silence lie motionless in his bed thinking over and over about the conversation they should have shared that fateful night. The one when he told his wife it was too dangerous to venture out. The one when he firmly and resolutely refused to take the risk on the treacherous road. The conversation he would regret for the rest of his life that they'd never had.

Some nights were worse than others and on the very worst the nightmares began the moment his head hit the pillow and ended as he sat bolt upright woken by either the ringing of the telephone or his alarm clock. Both signalling he should head in to the hospital, the only place that gave him purpose.

But this night he'd been woken from his tortured sleep by the sound of a falling branch outside his window. The weight of the snowfall had been too much for the narrow branch and it had snapped, crushing against the leadlight window. It had not broken the glass, merely scratched down the panes as it fell, making a noise not unlike a dying animal's scream.

Still damp with sweat, Charlie rushed to the window believing an injured deer might have roamed into his property, but he quickly saw the silhouette of the damaged tree lit by the moon. There were no streetlights as Charlie's home was on a large estate. The seven-bedroom, seventeenth-century, run-down and previously unloved manor home was undergoing much-needed renovations so he was sleeping downstairs on the leather chesterfield in the sitting room while work was being completed on the upstairs part of the house.

The stone slate roof had been in a state of disrepair for too long and the ceilings had been damaged in most of the upstairs rooms. The master bedroom was due to be finished within a few days. The rooms were all empty and waiting to be filled with new furniture although Charlie had no burning desire to see any of it, let alone choose it, so he had left those decisions up to the decorator. He wasn't rushing to move back into the master bedroom. He had not shared it with anyone for two years and he had no plans of sharing it again. His wife, Alice, had begun the renovations and he was seeing them through to completion in her honour. After that he did not know what he would do with the home.

Or himself, for that matter. Other than work, he had no plans for the future.

As always, once Charlie had been woken he found it hard to fall back into a sound sleep again. He read for a while and then tried once again to sleep. But slumber evaded him so he slipped on his heavy winter dressing gown, tied it loosely around his hips, headed into his kitchen and made himself a coffee. While memories of the accident monopolised his dreams, it was the impending arrival of the Australian *in-utero* surgeon that dominated his waking thoughts, leaving him both anxious and irritated about her potential interference.

The hospital's decision, or more precisely Assistant Head of Obstetrics, Oliver Darrington's decision, to fly the specialist over to consult infuriated him. In Charlie's opinion there was nothing to be gained and everything to lose. The quadruplets were only weeks away from being big enough to deliver and, as the attending OBGYN, Charlie thought any deviation from the treatment plan should be his decision. *In-utero* surgery carried risks that he did not consider warranted. And he wouldn't readily agree with the procedure without proof it was the best way forward.

As he looked out over what many would call a joy of the Cotswolds at Christmas, the majestic sight of dawn breaking over the snow-capped hillside, Charlie barely noticed any of the landscape. With his blood pressure beginning to rise, he sat down at the large oak kitchen table, sipping the coffee that was warming his fingers.

Dr Charlie Warren was unable to appreciate anything because he was preparing himself for a professional battle.

This time his words of caution would be heard. And heard loudly.

'What on earth do you mean, *there's no need for me to scrub in*?'

Juliet Turner spun around with confusion dressing her brow and a surgical gown covering her petite frame. 'My patient's on the operating table, prepped for an open foetal repair of a neural tube defect. I *have* to scrub in. This can't be postponed.'

'It hasn't been postponed, Dr Turner,' the theatre nurse told her. 'The surgery's going ahead today. It's just that you're not the surgeon operating.'

Juliet's nostrils flared behind the operating mask. 'That's even more ridiculous. There has to be a mistake.'

'No mistake, Dr Turner. Another *in-utero* specialist has been brought in to take over,' the nurse replied firmly. 'He's already arrived, and in gowning now. Orders came from further up the food chain than me, so don't go shooting the messenger.'

'*He's* in gowning! I'm sorry, Angie, but this is absolute nonsense,' Juliet said as she returned her focus to lathering her hands and forearms as a visible protest. She wasn't backing down and had no intention of relinquishing her role. Kelly Lester would have her surgery and her baby would have the best chance of a normal life. And she was operating as scheduled.

Being a female in a male-dominated profession had taught her to stand up for herself very early on. She had known entering the profession that women were at least twice as likely to drop out of surgical training programmes as men, making her well aware that it would not be an easy path and a shrinking violet would not succeed. During her studies her father, also a surgeon in the same field, often told her that, while half of the medical students in Australia and New Zealand were female, women made up less than ten per cent of fully qualified surgeons. It was a harsh reminder that she would have to be strong, focused and have a voice to survive. And she was going to use her voice whenever needed. Loud and clear.

It appeared that day was going to be one of those occasions.

'I will not allow another surgeon to just step in now without a damned good reason. I know this is not at the patient's request. I spoke to her only an hour ago.'

'No, it wasn't the patient who has requested the change, Dr Turner, and I understand you're taken aback but I'm just passing on the message, not making the decision. However, I'm telling you the decision's final. You really do need to stop scrubbing. Having sterile hands won't change the outcome.'

Not hiding her irritation, Juliet turned off the flow of water with the foot control. 'Well, we'll just see about that.'

'On the bright side, your replacement will no doubt meet with your approval. You've worked together more than a few times.'

Juliet was doubly confused with the smirk on Angie's face. None of it made any sense but if she was to believe the nurse, and she had no reason to doubt her, she was being replaced without notice or reason. 'I don't care who's been brought in to take over, it's still madness,' Juliet replied as she pulled her surgical cap free and the mass of brown curls dropped around her face. At that moment, the replacement doctor entered the scrub room.

'Really,' she announced, shaking her head in disbelief. 'This is becoming more and more ludicrous by the minute. They call you back here two days after you retire. What is this craziness? I've a patient about to be anaesthetised and I'm told I'm not operating. Will someone please explain the absurd rationale behind all of this? And who made the call to replace me as Kelly's surgeon?'

'The hospital director…but with good reason,' he replied.

'I can't think of one.'

'You have to prepare for your trip.'

Juliet paused for a moment with a perplexed stare. 'For goodness' sake has everyone gone completely mad? My trip's not until the middle of next week. I've got five days to prepare for the lectures and board the plane, but Kelly's baby needs this operation now if he's to ever walk.'

'That's where you're wrong…not about Kelly and her baby—you're right on that one, I just finished reading the notes and the surgery's urgent—but your trip's not next week. It's tomorrow. You're leaving on an eight o'clock flight in the morning.'

'Tomorrow? But why?' Juliet dropped her head into her hands still damp from the antibacterial wash. 'The lecture is not until next Thursday.'

'You're not delivering the lecture in Auckland...you're off to the UK—'

'The lecture's been cancelled?' she cut in.

'No, the lecture is going ahead...'

'But without me?' she asked as she pulled free her surgical gown and dropped it unceremoniously in the bin alongside her discarded cap.

'Yes.'

'And the surgery's proceeding too, just without me?' They were framed as questions but Juliet's tone made it obvious they were statements that she was none too happy about.

'That's right.'

'And I'm off to the UK?' she continued with the volume of her voice escalating and increasing in speed with each word. 'Before I go completely loopy, just tell me why my schedule is changing before my eyes without my approval?'

'The call came through from Cheltenham just now.'

'Cheltenham? As in the Cotswolds?'

'One and the same.'

'And who over there's making decisions without consulting with me?'

'The decision was made by four babies.'

Juliet blinked and shook her head. 'Four? You're speaking in riddles and you know that frustrates me.'

'Apparently the Assistant Head of Obstetrics at Teddy's, which is the maternity wing of the Royal Cheltenham hospital, spoke with our Head of Obstetrics about the quads. Almost twenty-nine weeks' gestation, suffering twin-to-twin transfusion syndrome. Two sets of monozygotic twins. While the girls are fine at this stage, the boys have developed the TTTS. Oliver Darrington believes you're the best chance that the quads have of all surviving should the parents agree to the *in-utero* laser surgery. And Professor Le Messurier just approved your secondment.'

'That's all very flattering but why am I being called in at the eleventh hour? If there was a risk, I should've been consulted upon the initial diagnosis. Surely being quads they would have been having weekly scans and intense monitoring and they'd know at Teddy's that the earlier the intervention, the better the outcome.'

'Apparently the quads were being closely monitored throughout the pregnancy, but the TTTS diagnosis has only just been made,' her replacement continued as he began scrubbing in, and over the sound of the running water he continued his explanation. 'The girls have separate placentas while the boys have one shared placenta so they were being scrutinised for any signs of transfusion. Up until now there was no indication of anything being amiss. It was picked up when the patient presented in what she thought was premature labour.'

'Caused by the amniotic fluid imbalance affecting the recipient twin.'

'Again, apparently but you'll know more details when you get there.'

'But the lecture in Auckland?'

'Handled. I'm not sure who's your proxy but your focus needs to be on the quadruplets. Darrington's worried it could deteriorate quickly and there's an increased risk they could lose at least one of them if you don't get over to Teddy's immediately, and of course we know the risks if one dies to the remaining foetuses. The parents have been briefed and want to be fully informed so they can consider *all* options, in particular the *in-utero* surgery.'

'Anything else I need to know?'

'Just one thing…the attending OBGYN, Dr Charlie Warren, is averse to fetoscopic laser surgery. Believes the risks are too great so no doubt he'll be challenging you.'

Juliet took a deep breath. 'Looks like I'll be catching a plane tomorrow morning to meet Dr Warren's challenge and convince him otherwise.'

'I hope he knows what he's up against.'

'He soon will.' With her head tilted just slightly, and the remnants of bewilderment still lingering, she looked at her replacement. 'Okay, Dad, looks like Kelly and her baby are in your hands now.'

'Don't worry, honey. I'll do you proud.'

CHAPTER TWO

'DR TURNER, WE'RE about five minutes away from the Royal Cheltenham hospital.'

The voice of the immaculately suited driver made Juliet lift her tired eyes to meet his in the rear-view mirror. They were warm and smiling back at her but with a curiosity that she had been so very accustomed to over the years. She was well aware that she didn't look her thirty-three years and many apparently found it difficult to believe she was a doctor let alone a surgeon. Her curly brown hair and spattering of freckles along with her petite frame, she realised, didn't help her quest to be taken seriously. She had no time for make-up except for a natural lip gloss to prevent her lips from cracking, and that too added to her young appearance. It also helped her go under the radar and not gain the attention of the opposite sex and, although it wasn't her primary motivation, it was a welcome side effect.

But despite the general consensus, she was both a surgeon and a mother and she took both roles incredibly seriously. Her work, she loved with a passion, and her daughter, she loved more than anyone and anything in the world. And more than she had ever dreamed possible.

'Thank you,' she responded as she gently turned to stir the little girl fast asleep and leaning against her. Running her fingers down the child's ruddy cheeks, she softly kissed the top of her head. 'Wake up, Bea, my precious little sleepyhead.'

The little girl silently protested at being disturbed and nestled in tighter to the warmth of her mother's woollen overcoat. Her eyelashes flickered but her eyes were far too heavy to open.

'Well, I hope this part of your marathon travel's been pleasant,' the driver commented.

'Very pleasant, thank you.'

'So how many hours have you two been travelling to be here this morning?'

'I think it's about thirty five hours, but it feels like for ever,' she replied with a little sigh, thinking back over the logistical nightmare they had survived. 'We left Perth early yesterday, Australian time, had a layover in Singapore before we headed on to Heathrow, and then the sixty-mile trip to the Cotswolds with you,' Juliet added as she continued to try and wake her still-drowsy little girl as gently as possible. She wasn't sure just how coherent she was but didn't want to appear rude. She had a lot on her mind, including the impending *in-utero* surgery on the quadruplets within the week. The reason she had been seconded halfway around the world at a minute's notice.

Keeping all four babies viable was everyone's focus. And something everyone agreed could not be done with Juliet on the other side of the world. Well, almost everyone agreed. She knew she would have her work cut out convincing the quads' OBGYN, Dr Charlie Warren. She presumed he would be leaning towards bed rest, high-protein diet and medication for the quads' mother. It was conservative and Juliet was surprised that he was not encouraging the laser surgery. She'd had no time to research the man but assumed he might be perhaps closer to the driver's age and had managed previous TTTS cases in that manner. But once he heard her argument for the surgery, surely the traditional English physician would see that her method had clear benefit? Particularly once she stated her case and the supporting statistics. How could he not? With both hospitals agreeing that Juliet was best placed to undertake the procedure, all she needed was the parents' approval. She was not about to allow Teddy's overtly conservative OBGYN to question the validity of her surgical intervention. It was an argument she was more than prepared to have. And to win.

But that wasn't the issue that had weighed most heavily on her mind on the long flights over to the UK. It was her parenting. How responsible was it to drag her daughter with her? she had wondered incessantly. And with less than twenty-four hours' notice. The poor little girl barely knew what was happening. The only thing that she could really comprehend was a plane trip to see snow.

Up until that point Juliet and Bea's lives had been so settled and planned. Some might say overly so, and among those were Juliet's parents. They had openly encouraged her to take Bea with her and together enjoy the opportunity to travel. In her home town, Juliet's mother looked after Bea three days a week and the other two days Bea was in childcare only five minutes from Juliet's workplace at the Perth Women's and Children's Medical Centre. When the proposition of travelling to the UK had been forced upon her, Juliet's parents had quickly had to push her out of her comfort zone and into embracing the opportunity. Her mother had immediately brought the suitcases down from the attic and personally delivered them to Juliet's home and offered to help her pack. Juliet didn't doubt it would be better for the quads for her to be there but it was not just *her* any more. She had her daughter to consider in every decision she made.

'I just hope I'm doing the right thing in dragging Bea to the other side of the world for such a short time,' Juliet had muttered in the car on the way to the airport at five-thirty in the morning. Her father had been driving, her mother next to Bea in the back seat.

'That's just it, honey, it might not be a short time,' her father reminded her as he pulled up at traffic lights and turned to his daughter. 'You don't know when the quads will arrive and it's best you stay until they do. There could be post-operative or postnatal complications, so it's better to remain there up to the birth.'

'I know you're right, but this whole trip is so rushed, I've had no time to prepare mentally. I know it's too late, but I can't hide the fact I'm having second thoughts about everything.'

'It's an amazing opportunity to consult at Teddy's and no one can come close to your level of expertise,' he said with pride colouring his voice as the lights changed and he took off down the highway. 'It's part of a teaching hospital, and along with assisting those four babies, not to mention their mother, you can add value to the students', interns' and residents' learning experience. You're the best in your field, Juliet. And I should know since I've operated alongside you more than once. It's time you took your skills out to the world, not just in research papers and journals and lecture tours, but in person in an operating theatre.'

'Dad, you're completely biased.'

'Nonsense, your father's right. We're both proud of you and you need to take that knowledge and expertise where it's needed most. Those babies and their parents need you,' her mother argued from the back seat. Her voice was soft but her tone was firm. Gently she kissed the top of her granddaughter's head. 'While we'd love to have Bea stay with us if it was for your three-day trip to Auckland, this is not three days. Poor little thing, she would fret terribly without you for any longer than a few days and visiting the UK will be such a wonderful experience for her too. It will be her first white Christmas.'

'And mine,' Juliet said, but her tone lacked her mother's enthusiasm as she drummed her fingers nervously on the leather upholstered seat. There was an uneasiness stirring in the pit of her stomach.

'Exactly, so stop questioning your decision. It's made now, you're both going,' her father piped up as he took the turnoff to Perth International airport in the dawn light. 'You've been hiding away, Juliet. You're not the only professional woman who's going it alone as a single mother. It's not the eighteen hundreds, and you don't need a man to help you realise your dreams. You have your career and Bea.'

She was hardly *going it alone*, in her opinion, with all of the help her parents provided, she thought as she looked out of her window and up into the still-darkened sky. But her father was right, she mused. She didn't need a man to experience or enjoy life. She and Bea would be just fine on their own. The plane would be up in that same sky in less than two hours, the sun would be up and they would be heading off to the other side of the world. To see four babies…and snow.

Juliet tried to muster a smile for everyone's sake. Her parents were always forthcoming with their very modern wisdom and they were generally right about everything. The quads needed surgical intervention and Bea needed to be with her mother. And Juliet could hardly stand being away from her daughter for a day, let alone the possibility of three or four weeks. So if Juliet went, then so would Bea.

Initially she wasn't sure how she would manage but when the information had arrived via email the night before, providing the details of the onsite hospital crèche, it had given Juliet no valid reason not to say yes to everything. Besides which, the tickets had been arranged. There was no turning back. And so it was that, with less than a day's notice, Juliet and Bea had left their sunburnt homeland behind and were on their way to Teddy's.

'It's a beautiful part of the world,' the driver announced, bringing Juliet back to the present. 'I've lived here for almost thirty years. Raised my children and now my grandchildren. You'll be sure to love it too.'

Juliet smiled at the way the man praised his home town. 'I won't be here quite that long, but long enough to enjoy the stunning scenery.' She looked out from the car window across fields blanketed in snow and dotted with trees and bushes in variant shades of green, all dusted by a fresh layer of white drift along the fences. It was so picturesque and a very long way from the long hot summer days of home. Since she could not turn back she had decided that she needed to accept her decision and be excited to share her first white Christmas with Bea. While she knew it had the potential to be a stressful time for her, with the impending surgery she would be performing, she was glad the two of them were together. They were like two musketeers off on an adventure.

Juliet had long accepted there would never be a third musketeer in their lives and that suited her fine. She didn't need a man in her life. Apart from her father, the rest just brought grief. Even in a new country, a man she had not laid eyes upon, Dr Charlie Warren's objection to her surgical option was another piece of proof that men caused unnecessary anguish.

And she didn't need any more of that.

'So you're only here for a short visit, then?'

'I'm consulting at Teddy's for a few weeks. I agreed because it was a short term. I couldn't keep my daughter away from her grandparents for too long. They'd miss her terribly.'

'I can see why. She's a proper little sweetie,'

the man added, clearly wanting to keep the conversation flowing.

Juliet guessed him to be in his mid-fifties. He looked a little like her father, quite distinguished, greying around his temples with a moustache and fine-rimmed gold glasses. Her father was a chatty man too, even in the operating theatre. Perhaps it was his age that made it easy for her to talk to this man. There was no hidden agenda. Just pleasant conversation.

'Thank you. She's my little angel and she's a real sweetie.'

'She's got your curls and pretty eyes. I don't think her father got much of a look-in there. My granddaughter's just the same, spitting image of her mother.'

Juliet felt her stomach sink a little, the way it always did at the mention of Bea's father. The man who had caused more anguish than she had ever thought possible. A man who didn't want *a look-in*. He was the one time she had let down her guard and the reason she would never do it again. After the one romantic night they had shared, he had walked away and never looked back. Married the fiancée he had forgotten to mention to Juliet while he was seducing her. And as quickly as he had swept into her life, he was gone. Well before she had discovered she was having his baby. Two months after the night they spent together, Juliet had caught sight of his wedding photo complete with huge bridal party in the society pages of the local newspaper.

She had instantly felt overwhelmingly sad for his new wife.

Heaved twice with morning sickness.

And sworn off men.

For ever.

Juliet paid the driver and asked him to take her bags to the boutique hotel where she was staying for a few nights. The hospital had contracted the car service and, after their conversation, she felt she could trust him to take her belongings, including Beatrice's pink fairy princess suitcase, and leave them with the hotel concierge. Being over fifty meant he fell in the trustworthy category. Men under forty had no hope in hell of being trusted with anything belonging to Juliet.

Not her suitcases…her medical decisions… or her heart.

With Juliet holding Bea's gloved hand tightly, the two of them stepped inside the warmth of the main entrance of the hospital to hear the heart-warming sound of piped Christmas carols. Juliet slipped off her coat and laid it over her arm and then unbuttoned Bea's as she watched her daughter's eyes widen at the sight of their surroundings. Teddy's, as the hospital was affectionately known, was certainly dressed in its Christmas best. Neither Juliet nor Bea had seen such a huge tree and certainly not one as magnificently decorated as the one that filled the glass atrium. It was overflowing with brightly coloured baubles, and tiny lights twinkled from behind the gold tinsel generously covering the branches. Their eyes both scanned around the foyer to see a Santa sleigh and carved wooden reindeers welcoming patrons to the hospital tea room and all the staff appeared as happy as both Juliet and Bea felt at that moment.

'Ith very beautiful, Mummy.'

'It is indeed.'

Taking hold again of her tiny daughter's hand, Juliet approached the information desk and introduced herself and mentioned her appointment with the OBGYN with whom she would be working.

'I'm sorry, Dr Turner, but Dr Warren hasn't arrived yet. He was due an hour ago but, to be honest, I haven't heard anything so I can't be sure what time we'll see him.'

Juliet's expression didn't mask her surprise. She had flown almost eight thousand miles and had arrived on time and Dr Charlie Warren, whom she assumed to be a resident of the Cotswolds and who therefore had a significantly shorter journey, was the one late for their meeting. She was not impressed and hoped he had a darned good explanation since she and Bea were each in need of a bath and some sleep and had gone without both to meet with him.

'Is Oliver Darrington available, then?'

'Mr Darrington's on surgical roster today so, I'm sorry, he won't be available until after four-thirty.'

Juliet was trying to think on her feet. And both her feet and her brain were tired. 'Then while we're waiting for Dr Warren perhaps I can take my daughter to the crèche.'

'Of course, that's on this floor but the other side of the building overlooking the visitor gardens,' the young woman told her. 'If you follow the corridor on your left to the end then turn right, you'll see it.' Then smiling, she added, 'And hear it. It's quite the noisy place with all the little ones.'

Juliet hesitated; she didn't want to walk away with Bea and have Dr Warren arrive. She checked her mobile phone for messages. Perhaps Dr Warren had been delayed and sent the hospital a message that hadn't reached Reception but had been relayed to her in a text. It seemed logical and it would give her an indication of how much time she had to settle Bea into the crèche, but after quickly finding her phone she discovered there was no such message.

'I suppose I shouldn't be surprised,' she muttered under her breath. 'Another unreliable man.'

'Pardon, Mummy?'

Juliet looked down at the angelic face staring back at her. 'Nothing, sweetie, Mummy was just mumbling. Everything's just perfect.'

'Okay,' Bea replied as her eyes darted from one festive decoration to the next before she began pulling her mother back in the direction of the main doors.

Juliet knew everything in their lives was not perfect but she would make it as perfect as she could for her daughter. She would devote her life to ensuring that Bea never felt as if she was missing out on anything. Particularly not about the lack of a father in her life. Juliet often felt sad that, while she enjoyed a wonderful relationship with her own father, Bea would never experience that bond. Although, she conceded gratefully, while the special father-daughter relationship would never be a part of her daughter's life, an unbreakable grandfather-granddaughter relationship had already formed. Juliet's father and Bea were like two peas in a pod and seeing that closeness brought Juliet joy.

She was drawn back to the current situation, caused again by a man. Bea's grip was tight and she was clearly on a mission as she tried to pull Juliet along. Juliet tugged back. 'It's so cold outside, darling. Let's stay in here where it's nice and warm.'

'But, Mummy, it lookth like the top of my cake.'

'What looks like the top of your cake, sweetie?'

'Out there,' the excited little girl replied as she pointed to the snow-covered ground. The branches of the trees and even the cars that had been parked for a few hours had been blanketed.

Juliet had to agree that it did look like Bea's fourth birthday cake. Her grandmother had baked a triple-layer strawberry sponge cake with a generous covering of brilliant white icing and decorated with four different fairy tale princesses for her beloved granddaughter. But this was not a cake, it was their reality for the next few weeks, and, despite her reservations and her annoyance with Charlie Warren, it was very pretty. Postcard pretty. And it was the first time either of them had seen snow up close and she couldn't blame her daughter for wanting to go outside and enjoy it.

'But I need to stay inside and wait for the doctor. He'll be here any minute, *I hope*, and I don't want to miss him when he arrives because after my meeting with him you and I can go to the hotel and have a nice nap.'

'*Pleeease* can I play in the snow?'

Juliet felt the sleeve of her blouse being tugged by two tiny hands, still gloved, and Bea's eyes were wide with anticipation and excitement. Juliet looked out to the fenced area near the entrance doors. There was a park bench, see-saw and a small slide and the playground was secured with a child safety gate. It was clearly a designated area for children to play on a sunny day but it wasn't a sunny day. It was freezing cold, overcast and the ground was covered with snow, which she knew was the draw card for Bea but a cause for concern for Juliet. Although she didn't want to impose a fear of almost everything onto her daughter, she couldn't help but worry.

After a moment she took a deep breath; she had made her decision. 'All right, you can play outside but only if we button up your coat again, put on your hat and keep your gloves on…and only for five minutes. And I mean five minutes—you'll catch a terrible cold if you stay out any longer.'

'Yeth! Yippee! Thank you, Mummy.'

With trepidation, Juliet buttoned up her daughter's heavy overcoat, pulled a knitted cap from her bag and popped it over Bea's mass of honey-blonde curls, pulling it down over her ears, and then slipped on her own coat again before walking the little girl outside into the wintry weather. She was still worried about leaving Bea for even five minutes, but common sense told her it would be safe. It was ten o'clock in the morning not the middle of the night and it was no longer snowing.

Her father's words rushed back into her head, 'You can't keep Bea in bubble wrap. Let her have some fun sometimes or she'll grow up scared of taking chances. Who knows what she can do in life if she's allowed to really live it? She might even become a surgeon like her mother…and grandfather.'

Although Juliet loved her work, she wasn't convinced medicine was the life she wanted for her daughter. Part of her wondered if the lack of a social life due to the years of heavy study load, and then the long shifts at the hospital as an intern, then as a resident didn't assist Bea's father to deceive her. She was far from streetwise about men. She'd had friends but never a love interest until she met him and he'd swept her off her feet and into his bed. Making her believe their night together was the beginning of something more. She wanted Bea to be wiser and not naive about the opposite sex.

But that was many years away and this was a playground. But it was still making Juliet very nervous.

She paused at the playground gate and looked down at her daughter, trying unsuccessfully to mask her concern.

'Mummy, I'll be good, I promith.'

Juliet realised she was being silly. It was only a children's playground and one she could see from inside and so too could all of the staff in the hospital foyer and the tea room. Juliet needed to meet with the now quite late Dr Warren. There might be a message from him any minute. She also wanted to meet the quadruplets' mother as soon as possible to discuss her treatment plan. Bending down and looking Bea in the eyes, she said, 'Mummy has to talk with the nice lady at the desk inside. I'll be back in five minutes. You know my rule—don't talk to strangers.'

Bea nodded. 'Okay.'

With that Juliet closed the childproof gate with Bea inside the playground wearing an ear-to-ear smile, already making small snowballs with her tiny gloved hands. Juliet tugged again on the gate to check it was closed properly before she headed back inside. She doubted she would leave Bea for five minutes, estimating it would only take two to check again on Dr Warren's whereabouts and see if there had been an update on his ETA. And she would be watching her the entire time through the large glass windows.

Charlie Warren pulled into the Royal Cheltenham hospital astride his black motorcycle. Both he and the bike were geared for riding in the harsh winter conditions of the southern English countryside. The sound of the powerful engine reverberated across the grounds as he cruised into the sheltered area of the car park. Charlie climbed from the huge bike that would have dwarfed most men, but, at six feet one, his muscular frame dressed in his leather riding gear stood tall against the bike. He removed his snow-splattered black helmet and heavy riding gloves and ran his still-warm fingers through his short but shaggy blond hair. It was cold riding to work every day, even brutal his colleagues would tell him some days in the middle of winter, but Charlie wouldn't consider for a moment taking a car. He couldn't; he didn't own one. Not any more and not ever again. He hadn't driven a car of any description in the two years since the crash.

Two years and three days to be exact. The anniversary was only a few days earlier, and, he assumed, was the reason the nightmares had returned. He knew he would never forget the date. It was the day the life he loved had ended.

After that, little brought him joy outside his work.

He had nothing to look forward to each night he rode away from the hospital. So he didn't stay away from Teddy's for too long.

Juliet watched Bea giggling as she climbed carefully up each rung of the tiny ladder on the slide. Her gloved hands gripped on tightly, her tiny feet, snug inside her laced-up leather boots, struggled a little not to slide, but she still smiled a toothy grin at her mother. Juliet loved seeing her daughter so happy and she smiled back but her smile was strained. Worry was building by the minute as she watched her only daughter take each slippery step, but her father's words resonated in her head, forcing her to stay put. Reminding her not to run to her daughter or call out, *Climb back down...it's dangerous*.

No, on this trip she would heed his instructions and let her daughter have a bit of fun after all and the slide was only a few feet tall.

What could possibly go wrong?

Bea looked down at each rung then back to her mother. Juliet could see that Bea thought she was such a big girl and seeing that reinforced that her father did know best. Juliet had to let Bea try new things. She had to unwrap the cotton wool that she had lovingly placed around her daughter...but only just a little.

Juliet gave a little sigh and resigned herself to her four-year-old's growing independence and her desire to encourage it but her fear at the same time. She wondered how she would cope when she turned sixteen and asked to get her driver's permit. Mentally she shook herself. *That's twelve years away...you have time to prepare for it*.

With any luck Dr Warren would arrive before then, she sniggered to herself.

At that moment, a smiling Bea lifted her right hand and waved at her mother. But Juliet didn't have time to smile back as she watched in horror as Bea lost her concentration and then her footing. She gasped out loud as her daughter's tiny hands lost their grip too. Helplessly Juliet watched from inside the building as Bea fell backwards to the ground.

CHAPTER THREE

CHARLIE SAW THE small child fall from the playground equipment. He was only too aware that while there was a thick blanket of freshly fallen snow in some places, in other areas there was only a thin covering. The shade the trees gave in summer when they were covered in lush green leaves was lovely but the branches had acted as natural canopies preventing the snow from building up to a level that would have broken her fall. He felt a knot in the pit of his stomach at seeing the child lying motionless on the ground and he rushed across the car park.

While it wasn't an overly tall slide, the child, he could see, was very tiny. As he drew closer he could see there was no one with her. Why would anyone leave a child out in the freezing weather unattended? He looked around and there was no one in sight. No one running to help. Fuelled by concern for the child and anger at the parent or parents, he raced to the gate.

'How damned irresponsible,' he muttered under his breath and shook his head. But his words were driven by something deeper. His dreams of being a father had ended the day his wife died and that made it even harder to see that this child had been left alone. If he were the father he would protect his child at any cost and he would never have left one so tiny out in the cold. Alone.

He undid the safety latch with a sense of urgency as he heard soft moans coming from the child he could then see was a little girl, lying still on her side. She was conscious. He quickly crossed to her and knelt down. 'You'll be okay, honey. I'm a doctor at this hospital. I just want to see if you've been hurt.' He kept his words to a minimum as he could see just how young she was.

'Where'th Mummy? I want Mummy.' Bea's eyes suddenly widened and began to fill with tears.

'We'll try and find Mummy,' he said as he wondered the very same question.

Where the hell was the little girl's mother? And her father?

As he began to check her vital signs he

guessed she was between three and four years of age. 'Where does it hurt?'

'My arm hurths,' she said, abruptly sitting upright with tears running down her ruddy cheeks.

Charlie was surprised but relieved to see her level of mobility and suspected her tears were fuelled by fear and pain in equal amounts. 'Anywhere else?'

'No. It'th jutht my arm. Where'th Mummy?' Her chin was quivering and the tears were flowing freely.

Charlie reassured her again they would find her mother as he continued his medical assessment. As she awkwardly tried to climb to her feet, it was obvious to Charlie that she had only injured her arm so he scooped her up ready to take her to the emergency department. Neither a stretcher nor a paramedic team was needed and he wanted to get her out of the bitter cold air immediately and into the warmth of the hospital where she could be thoroughly assessed.

'Put my daughter down now!' Juliet's loud voice carried from the gate to where Charlie was standing.

Charlie's eyes narrowed on her. 'I'm a doctor, so please open the gate for me and step aside. This child's been hurt,' he told her as he approached with Bea still firmly in the grip of his strong arms. 'I'm taking her to have an X-ray.'

Juliet hurriedly opened the gate. 'She's my daughter. I can take her,' she said, reaching out for Bea, but Charlie ignored her request and moved swiftly, and in silence, in the direction of the emergency entrance with Juliet running alongside him.

'I said, I can carry her.'

'I heard you but I have her, so let's keep unnecessary movement to a minimum.'

Juliet nodded. It was logical but she still wished her injured daughter were in her arms, not those of the tall, leather-clad stranger who was supposedly a doctor. 'I saw her fall but I couldn't get to her in time.'

Charlie's eyebrow rose slightly. 'That's of no consequence now. I saw her. I'll get her seen immediately in A&E and then you can perhaps explain why she was left unattended out in this weather at such a young age.'

'Excuse me?' Juliet began in a tone that didn't mask her surprise at his accusatory attitude. While she thought it was unfair and unjust it also hit a raw nerve. 'I wasn't far away—'

'Far enough, it would seem, for me to get to her first,' Charlie cut in with no emotion in his voice. As the three of them entered the warmth of the emergency department, the feeling between them was as icy as the snow outside. 'I need her name and age.'

'Beatrice, but we call her Bea, and she's four years and two months.' Juliet answered but her voice was brimming with emotion. Overwhelming concern about Bea and equally overwhelming anger towards the man who was carrying her child. How dared he be so quick to judge her?

'Four-year-old girl by the name of Bea, suspected green stick fracture of the forearm,' he announced brusquely to the nursing staff as he took long, powerful strides inside with Juliet following quickly on his heels. Charlie carried Bea into one of the emergency cubicles and laid her gently on the examination bed. With the curtains still open, he continued. 'We need an X-ray *stat* to confirm radius or ulna fracture but either way, if I'm correct, we'll be prepping for a cast. And bring me some oral analgesia.'

'Ibuprofen, acetaminophen or codeine?' the nurse asked.

'One hundred milligrams of suspension ibuprofen,' Charlie replied, then, as it was a teaching hospital and he was aware that three final-year medical students had moved closer to observe, he continued. 'Generally paediatric fracture patients have significantly greater reduction in pain with ibuprofen than those in either the acetaminophen group or the codeine group and they suffer less negative side effects.'

'What'th happening, Mummy?'

'The doctor,' she began before she shot an angry glare over her shoulder in Charlie's direction. She was impressed with his knowledge but not his attitude towards her. 'Sweetie, the doctor thinks you may have broken your arm when you fell from the playground slide so he'll take a picture of your arm with a special machine.'

'Will it hurt?'

'The machine won't hurt you at all but they will have to very gently lift your arm to take off your coat and then take a picture. So the doctor will give you some medicine so it doesn't hurt.'

The nurse returned with the ibuprofen and Charlie asked Bea to swallow the liquid.

'Please do as the doctor asks because it will make the pain go away,' Juliet told her daughter with a smile that belied how worried she was. 'Don't worry, Bea, I'll be with you every minute. I'm not leaving your side.'

'That'd be a nice idea,' Charlie put in, with

sarcasm evident in his voice just enough for Juliet alone to know the intent of his remark but no one else. Without looking up, he signed the radiograph request the A&E nurse had given him.

Juliet took a deep breath and counted silently to three. It was not the time to tell him just what she thought of his snide remarks, particularly not in the presence of her daughter and the medical students. But that time would come once everyone was out of earshot. And he would hear in no uncertain terms just what he could do with his unwarranted opinion.

'Can you please complete the paperwork?' the nurse asked of Juliet. 'We only need the signature of one parent.'

'Bea only has one parent,' Juliet said flatly before she accepted the clipboard from the nurse and hurriedly but accurately began to complete the details so she could expedite the process and allow Bea to have the X-ray. She wasn't sure if the doctor had heard and she didn't care as Bea's parental status wasn't his concern.

'Dr Warren,' another young nurse began as she neared the trio with a clipboard, 'would you like me to call for the paediatric resident so you can return to the OBGYN clinic?'

'No, I'm here now, I'll finish what I've started.'

'Of course,' the nurse replied. 'Then we can take the patient down as soon as the paperwork is completed.'

'Dr Warren? Dr Charlie Warren?' Juliet demanded as she fixed her eyes on Charlie for a moment. He was not the borderline elderly OBGYN she had pictured. Dr Charlie Warren, she surmised, was closer to his early thirties.

'Yes. Why do you ask?'

Juliet didn't answer immediately. Instead she ensured she had not missed any details on the admissions form before she signed and returned it to the nurse. It gave her a few moments to compose herself and reconcile that the man treating her daughter was the OBGYN who had stood her up for their meeting and the one who wanted to oppose her treatment plan for the quadruplets. He was already very much on the back foot but, with his obvious bad attitude, it did not augur well for them working together.

'Well, Dr Warren, it appears that you owe me an apology since you're the reason why my daughter is in here.' Juliet wore a self-satisfied look, one she felt she more than deserved to display.

'I hardly think so. I just pulled into the car park when your daughter fell. We both know that I had nothing to do with her accident so let's not waste time trying to shift blame. Leaving a child this young alone is something I am not sure I can fully understand… or want to.'

'That's where you're wrong. You have everything to do with the accident because if you'd been on time for our meeting my daughter would not have stepped outside to play.'

'Our meeting?'

'Yes, our ten o'clock meeting,' she began. 'I'm Dr Juliet Turner. The *in-utero* surgeon who has flown halfway around the world and managed to be here on time for a meeting about your quad pregnancy patient, and, I might add, we travelled straight from the airport. My daughter needed to stretch her legs for a minute after such a long journey, so I allowed her to play in the fenced area that I assumed would not be open unless it was in fact child-safe while I enquired further about your arrival. If heavy snowfall changes the safety status of the area then it should be closed. You may like to speak to the hospital board about looking into that matter.' Juliet had not taken a breath during the delivery.

Adrenalin was pumping out the words. She was scared for Bea. And extremely angry with Charlie Warren.

'Dr Turner? I had no idea…'

'Clearly…and apparently no time management either.'

Charlie was momentarily speechless. Juliet felt momentarily vindicated.

She noticed a curious frown dress his brow. Then she also noticed, against her will, that his brow was very attractive, as was his entire face. She had been focusing on Bea and not noticed anything much about the man who had whisked her daughter unceremoniously into A&E. But now she noticed his chiselled jaw, deep blue eyes and soft, full mouth. In fact, each moment her eyes lingered on his face she realised he was in fact extremely handsome, even when he frowned. His powerful presence towered over her with long, lean legs and his leather riding gear accentuated his broad shoulders. She shook herself mentally. His manner was both judgmental and conceited. Alarm bells rang in her head. Why were her thoughts even teetering on noticing him past being her daughter's emergency physician? He was just another arrogant man and one she was going to be forced to work with in some capacity.

In a perfect world she would have nothing to do with him once he had finished treating Bea. But she also knew that they didn't live in a perfect world. And not seeing Charlie Warren again wasn't possible. They would be consulting on the high-risk patient until the birth of the four babies.

And she was well aware that, after challenging her parenting, he would shortly be challenging her treatment plan. There was no way this working relationship was going to run smoothly. And she doubted with his attitude he intended to play nicely.

'I had additional house calls this morning as I needed to cover another OBGYN's patients. He's down with the winter virus that swept through Teddy's. With both patient loads it took longer than I anticipated, but point taken. I should have called in.'

Juliet couldn't help but notice him staring at her. It was a curious stare, no longer angry or accusing.

'I understand covering for ill colleagues happens but a text would have been prudent,' she continued, ignoring his reaction, suspecting like everyone else he was looking at her as if she weren't old enough to be a surgical specialist. She had grown tired of that look and in Dr Warren's case she wasn't about to give him any leeway. Nor was she about to give her unexpected reaction to him any acknowledgement. Her tone was brittle but with his masculinity hovering around eleven out of ten he was making it difficult not to be a little self-conscious despite her ire.

'We can speak further about my delay later, Dr Turner, but let's get Bea into Radiography and ascertain the extent of the fracture,' Charlie announced, breaking her train of thought.

Juliet did not respond to Charlie as she wasn't sure what exactly she would say. Her equilibrium was beyond ruffled and she was struggling to keep her thoughts on track. She returned her attention to Bea, and stroked her daughter's brow. 'Mummy and the doctor will be taking you on this special bed to have that picture now. And then if the doctor is right and you have broken the bone in your arm then you will have a cast put on until it's all healed.'

'What'th that?'

'You know when Billy, the little boy from playgroup, fell over last year and he had a bright blue plaster on his arm? And everyone drew pictures on it with crayons? That's a cast.'

Bea nodded. 'I drew a star and a moon.'

'That's right, and it was a very beautiful star and moon.'

'Can I take it off? Billy couldn't take it off.'

'No, you won't be able to take it off but it won't be too uncomfortable,' Charlie chimed in with a voice that Juliet noticed had suddenly warmed. She wasn't sure if that warmth was directed at Bea alone or if he was attempting to be nice to Juliet as well. 'There's a soft bit inside and a hard layer outside that stops your arm from moving so that it can heal.'

Juliet turned back to face Charlie to ask another question and immediately wished she hadn't. He had moved closer and his face was only inches from her. His cologne was subtle and very masculine. She tried to keep the same professional demeanour but dropped her eyes, refusing to keep the courtesy of eye contact for two reasons. One, she was still fuming and waiting for an apology that she doubted she would ever receive, and, two, she didn't want to risk falling into the dark blue pools that were more blue than any she had ever seen before. She didn't want to forgive him for his appalling behaviour. Without all of the facts he had jumped to a conclusion that was unjust. But her hormones were overriding her good sense. It was completely out of character for her. She was angry and she never paid attention to men, good-looking or not. And she would be damned if she would allow it to happen that day. Or any day in the future.

She quickly decided she didn't want to hear an apology from Charlie. If one was not offered it would mean that she could then remain furious with good reason, keep the man at arm's length and her mettle would not be tested. If he made amends, he might prove to be a distraction on some level that she didn't want. Although she knew her sensible side would win, she didn't want to waste any time on some ridiculous internal battle of hormones versus logic. Particularly when she had a very real battle to fight with the very same man.

Coughing, she cleared her throat in an attempt to gain some composure. Dr Warren's nearness was, for some inexplicable reason, threatening to awaken something in Juliet she had buried a long time ago. And it didn't need digging up now. That part of her life was over. Perhaps it was just sleep deprivation, she wondered. She had not travelled for so many hours straight before either. Nor had her daughter ever suffered an injury of that nature. It had to be the series of events stacked against her that was messing with her logic. Making her emotions a little unstable. It wasn't her. It definitely had to be the combination of factors, she decided, not Charlie Warren himself. Suddenly she had everything back in perspective, the way she liked it. Charlie Warren was her daughter's doctor and her potential nemesis.

'Will you be using fibreglass?' she asked, quieting any sign of emotion. Her heart was no longer beating madly and the butterflies were one by one exiting her stomach. She was proud of herself for so quickly once again gaining control of the situation. Although she was still disturbed the *situation* had presented in the first place.

Jet lag, she quickly told herself. Definitely jet lag.

'If Bea needs a cast we'll use fibreglass and, since it will be difficult to expect Bea to keep it dry, I'll use a waterproof lining too,' Charlie told her.

'Billy had blue but I don't like blue,' Bea said softly, looking down at her arm.

'We have pink and yellow and I think red too,' Charlie responded with his mouth curving to a half-smile and that did not go unnoticed by Juliet.

'I like red for Chrithmath…but pink ith pretty… I want pink,' Bea announced.

Juliet smiled at her daughter. As she lifted her head her eyes met Charlie's eyes staring back at her and her heart once again began to pick up speed. It was madness for certain. The intensity of his gaze wouldn't allow her to look away. It was as if there was something deeper, something hidden behind the outer arrogance. Warmth and kindness seemed almost trapped inside him.

And she couldn't ignore, no matter how much she didn't want it to be true, and how much she'd fought it over the years, that there was a tiny part of her craving warmth and kindness from a man like Charlie.

CHAPTER FOUR

'UNFORTUNATELY BEA HAS a distal radial fracture...but at least it's non-displaced so we should be grateful for that news.'

Charlie turned back from the radiographs on the illuminated viewer in the room to see Juliet holding her daughter closely. He could not help but notice the tenderness in her embrace and the obvious love Juliet had for her daughter. He had been wrong about her, he admitted to himself as he watched her gently kiss the mop of blonde curls on the top of her daughter's head. He had not accompanied them to the radiography department. Instead he had excused himself to change into street clothes he kept in his office and then met them back in the emergency department.

Their eyes met and he paused in silence for a moment. He hoped she had not noticed him staring longer than was necessary but he could not help himself. Despite their professional differences, there was something about Juliet that was making him curious. Making him want to know more about the single mother with the Australian accent; the very pretty face; the spitfire personality; and the adorable daughter. He had noted her mention Bea only had one parent. Whether she was widowed, divorced or had never married, he didn't know. And it was none of his business.

It was out of character for him to be distracted by anything or anyone. Least of all someone he had only just met. But he could not pretend even to himself that he had not been distracted by Juliet, and it was not just her appearance. She was a conundrum. A surgeon who looked closer in age to a first-year medical student while he knew she would have to be in her thirties, with an academic record that would come close to that of a professor and an attitude when provoked of a bull. Not to mention a love for her child that was palpable. He had not met anyone quite like Dr Juliet Turner before.

Charlie was never thrown by anyone or anything. Charlie Warren's life was organised and predictable. It was the only way he could function. He had few friends, save his colleagues during his work hours. Socialising was a thing of the past although he had been forced to attend the recent hospital fundraiser, escaping as soon as decently possible.

He spent any time away from the hospital alone and preferred it that way. In more than two years, Charlie had never experienced any interest in anything other than his work. Returning home only to sleep and prepare for the next day's surgery or consultations. His patients were his sole passion in life. And now the Australian *in-utero* expert, with whom he completely disagreed on a professional level, was rousing his curiosity in knowing more about her.

And it was unsettling.

The second anniversary of the accident had just passed and it was a day he wanted to do differently every night as he lay alone in his bed reliving the hell that had become his waking reality. One he couldn't change. One he had accepted a long time ago that he would live with for the rest of his life. And to be spending any time thinking about a woman other than his late wife was ridiculous.

But as much as he fought the distraction, he couldn't control his wandering thoughts.

He wondered for a moment what life had dealt Juliet. Just being a surgeon would have provided struggles along the way. He had found the study and workload gruelling and he was not raising a child alone. Whether or not her status as a single mother was recent he was unsure. She looked to him like a waif but she had the fire and fight of someone a foot taller and he assumed she would have faced life head-on. His wife had been similar in stature but very different in demeanour and profession. She was quietly spoken, and a local Cotswolds girl who managed a craft shop in town. She spent hours quilting and running the little store that doubled as a social hub for the local community.

Charlie doubted that Juliet would have any interest in quilting. But it bothered him greatly that questions about the woman holding her daughter had suddenly and unexplainably captured his thoughts.

He was grateful that Juliet had been distracted by the nurse coming back and looked away. For some unfathomable reason he was struggling to do just that. The woman before him was nothing close to the stoic surgical specialist he'd been expecting and he was shocked at just how much he had noticed about her in such a short space of time.

And he was angry and disappointed with himself for doing so.

* * *

Juliet forced herself to blink away her wandering thoughts. Charlie Warren was nothing closc to what she'd been expecting. His white consulting coat covered black dress jeans and blue striped shirt. He was still wearing his black motorcycle boots. The combination of the leather and gunmetal hardware of his boots was both edgy and masculine. It had to stop. She had not flown to another hemisphere to find herself distracted by the first handsome man she met. First handsome, *arrogant* man who would be her work colleague for the next few weeks.

She felt butterflies slowly returning just knowing he was so close to her. Close enough to reach out and touch her. Not that he would… nor would she want that, she told herself sternly. But it was as if she could see there was something more to the man who had rudely stood her up and then berated her for inattention to her daughtcr. Was his brash exterior a shield? She wasn't sure as she tried in vain to analyse the ogre. Perhaps it was the way he had rushed to Bea. As a man and as a doctor, he had not hesitated to help Juliet's daughter. He had lifted her into the safety and strength of his arms the way a father would. The way Bea's own father never would and the way no man other than her grandfather up until that day had done.

But it was romantic nonsense. He was just the tall and not so dark—more dusty blond—handsome stranger of happily ever after stories that she knew didn't really exist.

There wasn't anything more to this man, her practical self was saying firmly and resolutely despite how her body was arguing. He wasn't even nice let alone the type to sweep her off her feet. He was far too brusque and cold. What was going on in her tired mind? she wondered. It had to be international time difference setting in. Most definitely. It couldn't be anything else stirring her thoughts into chaos. She needed a good night's sleep and all would be as it should be. And she would be looking at her colleague as just that, a colleague. And if his strong, borderline obstinate opinion about her plans on surgical intervention with the quadruplets' mother remained, they would in fact shift from colleagues to adversaries.

She took solace in the idea that their differing opinions would add another protective layer to the armour she wore very comfortably.

'Hmm-hmm…' Juliet coughed. 'I said I'm happy there's no need for a closed reduction.'

'That makes two of us,' he replied, turning back to the radiographic films.

'So there'll be no intervention to realign the bones, just a cast as we already discussed, then?' Juliet continued as she fought to keep her thoughts professional.

'It's standard practice to give the arm a few days in a sling to allow swelling to subside,' Charlie explained to everyone in the room. 'But I'm concerned at Bea's age she may cause further damage if we don't protect the fracture with a cast. There's a marginal amount of swelling around the fracture site but not enough to warrant risking further damage by allowing it to be without protection.' He then asked the nurse to prepare for the cast while three medical students, who had quickly become part of the furniture, continued listening intently. The nurse moved swiftly, while the medication still kept Bea's pain at bay. 'And we need pink. That is the colour you want, isn't it, Bea?'

Bea looked up and nodded.

'Then pink it is,' he told her. The nurse helped Juliet to carefully roll up Bea's long-sleeved top that she had worn underneath the woollen jacket that was still under Juliet's arm.

'You were all layered up, weren't you,

young lady?' the nurse commented with a smile. 'Rugged up for our chilly winter?'

Bea nodded and watched as her mother and the nurse worked gently to lift the clothing free so the cast could be applied.

'It's a nice loose top so it should roll down again afterwards, but the jacket will never fit so we'll have to just rest that over her shoulders and go shopping for a cape,' Juliet mentioned as she dropped the little coat on the nearest chair.

Charlie began the process of applying the cast, explaining to Bea in simple language every step, while also including a short tutorial for the students' benefit as they stood observing the process from the sidelines. Juliet listened to the way he spoke so tenderly to her daughter and she felt the flutter of the annoying butterflies emerging once again. She hated the feeling but she was unable to control it. His manner and tone to Bea made him appear almost fatherly. She sternly told herself it had to be his standard bedside manner…but she wasn't completely convinced.

'Applying a cast is quite a simple procedure,' he began as he turned his attention to the students. 'I'll begin by wrapping several layers of soft cotton around the injured area. Today I'll be applying a short cast that extends from the wrist to just below the elbow as the break is a distal radial fracture so extending further than that would cause unnecessary discomfort to the patient.' Charlie worked at wrapping Bea's tiny injured arm, and as he spoke the fibreglass outer layer was being soaked in water. Gently he wrapped the fibreglass around the soft first layer. 'While the outer layer is wet at the moment, it will dry to a hard, protective covering. I'll make some tiny incisions in the cast to allow for any potential swelling.'

In less than thirty minutes, Beatrice Turner was the proud owner of a pretty pink cast. And her mother could not help but be impressed with the way in which Dr Charlie Warren had attended to her daughter, executed the delicate procedure and managed to deliver a tutorial to the students. All the while continuing to look devastatingly handsome. She shook herself mentally and tried to remind herself of his initial overbearing attitude. But it was difficult when he was displaying such empathy to the little person she loved most in the world.

'Now you need to rest this arm quite still for about an hour, Bea,' Charlie said. 'The nurse will keep an eye on it and we'll leave your top rolled up for the time being.'

Bea just looked at the cast. Her eyes told the story. They were filled with confusion. It had been an overwhelming experience for her and she wasn't taking in much of what was being said at that moment.

'And we can give you a sling to hold it up because it might get heavy over the next few weeks.'

Still Bea just sat in silence. Juliet suspected it was a combination of jet lag and the pain beginning to resurface.

'Mummy will be here,' she told her softly as she stroked her hair.

Juliet waited for another snide remark, in fact she hoped for one, but Charlie made none. She didn't like not having a reason to dislike the man.

'It may get itchy, Bea, and if it does you can tap on the outside and that might help, but don't put anything inside like a pencil because it might scratch your skin and we don't want germs in there.'

Juliet watched as Bea tilted her head slightly with a curious expression on her beautiful face. She knew her daughter was still a little confused by everything that had happened so quickly. It was a lot for a four-year-old to take in such a short amount of time.

'Is there anything else we can do?' Juliet

asked, holding Bea's free hand and quickly trying to recall her training in paediatric fractures during medical school. It had been so long since she had graduated from her general medical studies before specialising and she was stretching her memory.

'It would be best to sponge-bathe Bea so that the cast doesn't fill with water in the bath or shower. While the outside of the cast is waterproof, as you know, the inside isn't, even with the special lining. It needs to be kept dry, so no lotions or oils either.' He paused to recall the other instructions that once rolled off his tongue as an A&E resident. 'And if the itching starts to bother Bea, you can use a cool hairdryer to blow air in around the edge of the cast and check now and then that she hasn't hidden small toys or sweets inside the cast. Believe it or not, during my A&E rotation I had more than one child think of it as their secret *hideyhole*.'

'No doubt,' Juliet said with a smile that she hadn't thought previously she would ever display in Charlie's presence. Her defences were slowly melting as his bedside manner warmed the room. She began a mental inventory of Bea's belongings, wondering if she'd brought anything that small with her on the trip. She felt certain as she looked at the tiny gap that Bea's possessions would not fit inside.

'I'm sure you'll have it under control,' Charlie said to her before he turned his attention once again to the medical students. 'Along with asking the parents or caregivers to check the cast regularly for cracks, breaks, tears and soft spots, what else would you ask them to look out for and what would warrant medical attention?'

'Pain that doesn't get better with the prescribed pain relief,' one of the students offered.

'Yes, anything else?'

'If the child complains of feeling numb or tingly in the vicinity of the fracture,' another chimed in with a self-satisfied smile.

'Good.'

'Blisters inside the cast,' the third student said confidently, then continued, 'and fever, or any significant increase in temperature.'

While being a tutor was nothing new to Charlie, doing so back in A&E was a change of pace and very different subject content but he didn't want to exclude the students. 'Well done. You seem to have a good understanding of the basics of paediatric fractures.'

The A&E resident poked her head in at that moment and directed her conversation to the medical students. 'If you're finished here, there's suspected tetanus in bay three and gallstones in bay seven. Take your pick.'

Charlie grinned. 'It's been a while since I've heard a call for one of those conditions. It's usually onset of labour or unexplained abdominal cramps over in Teddy's.'

The three looked at Charlie for approval to leave, which he gave in a nod, and they left, as did the attending nurse, leaving Charlie and Juliet alone with Bea.

'Well, it looks as if we're all finished, then,' Juliet offered in a voice that did not give anything away about the effect Charlie was still having on her, being so near. His natural affinity with her daughter was thawing parts of her she wanted to remain frozen.

'I think we are.' His eyes once again locked on hers for just a minute but long enough to make her heart race just a little faster.

She swallowed nervously, growing more irritated with herself by the minute. Behaving like a schoolgirl experiencing her first infatuation was not her usual demeanour, nor one she intended to entertain. Not for another second. Reinstating herself as the quads' surgeon, not Bea's mother who had a borderline crush on her daughter's doctor and her own soon-to-be colleague, was a priority.

Biting her lower lip, she tried to channel someone very different from herself. A detached, bumptious persona she had created over the years when people looked at her like a child and they needed reminding of her medical credentials. And it would work perfectly at that moment. 'It's best, then, that we reschedule the *in-utero* surgical consultation that you missed earlier. If you can provide me with overnight obs about both the mother and babies, we'll be off to the hotel so Bea can rest and I can brief myself on their progression and return this afternoon.'

Her voice had suddenly morphed from warm to officious. And as she stood her relaxed posture had become stiff. Her body language screamed confrontation. But Charlie didn't appear to take the bait as he helped Bea down from the examination table. Although his tone returned once again to something more formal and detached.

'I'll email you the updates, Dr Turner.'

She felt she had been successful. The atmosphere in the room had cooled and for that she was grateful. It was just the way she wanted it.

'I appreciate that, Dr Warren.'

'Great, I'll leave you both in the A&E's care and head up to visit with Georgina and

Leo. They're waiting for my update on their babies' treatment plan, because since the diagnosis it appears the recipient twin is now struggling.'

Juliet froze on the spot. 'Georgina and Leo Abbiati? The quads' parents?'

'Yes.'

'But that's why I'm here. Why would you not include me in that consultation? And why would you not update me immediately?'

'Because you just excused yourself.'

'No, I didn't,' Juliet argued with her nostrils beginning to flare. 'I excused myself from *our* meeting. Not the meeting with the quads' parents. I thought that was scheduled for this afternoon.'

'It was, but yesterday I decided to bring it forward since the condition had deteriorated slightly. Which is what I just mentioned.'

'What exactly do you mean by "deteriorated slightly"?'

'There's more amniotic fluid so the uterus is almost at capacity. It might be a good idea to do an amniotic reduction.'

'I'll need to assess her immediately,' Juliet told him. 'And I wouldn't be considering the reduction if we are undertaking the laser surgery in a few days.'

'Whether the laser surgery will go ahead is still to be decided by the Abbiatis.'

'And without me, it would appear. Didn't you think that it would be nice to consult with me about treatment plans? I thought we would meet at *ten this morning*, you would brief me on the current viability of all four babies, the affected babies' condition and the mother's status and I would take that into consideration and then, with a consolidated treatment plan, meet with the parents late today.'

'I scheduled it for now as I thought you'd want to meet with the parents immediately.'

Juliet drew a deep breath. She needn't have worried she was warming to him because Charlie Warren had very quickly given her a cold shower when he'd returned to being a dictator with a medical degree. She wasn't sure if he had taken her cue or it was his intention all along but either way any attraction she had felt instantly disappeared.

Juliet had to think on her feet. She would not be made to appear less than professional by not attending the consultation. This was about the option of surgical intervention. Not Charlie Warren's conservative treatment plan. Waiting for the birth was not in her expert opinion the best way forward. The best chance was surgery to remove the offending artery and save all four babies and she wanted the Abbiatis to have all the facts before they made their decision.

'I want to meet with them as soon as possible.'

'Then let's go. I'm meeting with them in fifteen minutes.'

'What about Bea?'

Charlie looked down at Bea's little face and his heart began to melt. If life had been different he would have been looking at the face of his own child every night. He or she would have been younger than Bea but he and his wife had planned on children. Four of them if possible. Leaving the hospital every night to return to his wife and those much-loved children, to read them bedtime stories and tuck them in to sleep, was his dream but instead he returned to an empty house in the middle of renovations that he didn't care about. His life was as empty as his house.

And suddenly the daughter of the overbearing woman who shouldn't have any effect on him was doing just that. He wasn't able to define what made her special—perhaps it was because she was like a tiny angel with a broken wing. Although he did not feel her mother had fallen from heaven.

'I said, what do you propose I do with my

daughter?' Her voice was firm but not much more than a whisper. She didn't want Bea to feel she was in the way or not wanted.

'Bring her along to my office and I'll ask one of the nurses to keep an eye on her,' he told Juliet as he patted Bea's hand.

'I don't feel comfortable with that.'

'Then go home…'

'Go home?'

'I meant go back to the hotel and we'll arrange a second consultation tomorrow.' Charlie walked over and opened the door. 'We're all finished in here,' he told the nurse as he left A&E.

'So you won't postpone the consultation until this afternoon, then?' she asked, exasperated with his attitude and following slowly on his heels with Bea in tow.

'No, definitely not. Postponing has the potential to make both parents extremely anxious, not to mention Leo's taken time away from the family business to be here.' Charlie pressed the elevator button for OBGYN on the second floor and turned back to face her.

Juliet's gaze swept the hospital corridor as she rubbed her forehead. In her mind, the Abbiatis needed to be provided with both treatment plan options to consider. Charlie would no doubt suggest a 'wait and see' treatment plan or next propose medication as an option. After sleeping on it, the second option of surgical intervention, she conceded, would be the scarier of the two to Georgina and Loo. The delivery gap between both might sway them to what was not in their best interests. Nor the interests of the babies.

She felt trapped.

'Fine, we'll do it your way. I'll attend,' she said as the three of them stepped inside the empty elevator. 'But I'll need a few minutes to find the crèche and settle Bea in.'

'Fine, you have ten minutes.'

'Can't you delay the consultation for half an hour?'

'No.'

'No?' she repeated incredulously. 'Not, perhaps…or I'll see what I can do? Who made you the final decision maker? Oliver Darrington actually seconded me here, not you.'

'But I'm Georgina's OBGYN, so I make the final decision on this case. It's how we run it at Teddy's. Check with Oliver if you like, but he will without doubt defer to me.'

'I don't have time to chase down Mr Darrington.'

'Good because I'm already running behind.'

The doors of the lift opened into OBGYN.

The waiting room was full and all eyes turned to them. Charlie considered compromise was in everyone's best interest. 'I'll give you twenty minutes to settle Bea into the crèche, Dr Turner. Then I'll begin the Abbiatis' consultation in Room Two-Thirteen.'

With that, Charlie disappeared down the corridor leaving Juliet and Bea standing opposite the nurses' station. Juliet realised immediately that the middle ground he had offered had more to do with circumstance than generosity of spirit. The patients were all looking in their direction and had clearly been the impetus for the change in tone. She was well aware that he had the potential to be a medical ogre when out of earshot of others.

'Dr Turner?'

Juliet looked up to see a very pretty willowy blonde nurse smiling back at her. 'Yes.'

'Hi, I'm Annabelle Ainsley. I'm the head neonatal nurse,' the blue-eyed woman told her. 'We've been expecting you.'

Juliet guessed the nurse to be in her mid-thirties as she stepped out from behind the station with her hand extended.

'Juliet Turner,' she responded as she met her handshake.

'And who is this gorgeous young lady with the very pretty coloured cast?'

'My daughter, Bea.'

'Hello, Bea,' Annabelle said.

Bea gripped her mother's hand a little tighter as she looked up at the very tall nurse. Her long blonde hair was tied in quite a severe style atop her head that made her appear even taller.

'Pink's my favourite colour in the world,' Annabelle continued and bent down a little to come nearer to the little girl's height. 'I love it so much I even have pink towels and pink soap.'

Bea loosened her grip a little. 'Me too,' she replied with her toothy grin and then smiled up at her mother before she continued. 'I have a pink bed.'

'Yes, you do, and a pink quilt. In fact your room is a pink palace,' Juliet agreed.

'Wow, that's awfully special. I wish I had pink sheets and a pink quilt.'

Juliet was happy that Annabelle and Bea were engaging but she was becoming increasingly concerned about the timeframe she had to get to the consultation and she knew she was hiding the fact well.

'Is there something I can help you with?' Annabelle asked.

'Yes, actually there is. I need to find the crèche as soon as possible. Dr Warren and

I'll be meeting with the Abbiatis shortly and I need to settle Bea in, and I haven't had a chance to look over the last two days' obs for Georgina as I've been travelling—'

'I can help with all of that,' Annabelle cut in.

'You can? That would be wonderful. Thank you so much.'

'Not at all,' Annabelle replied with a smile. 'I've just finished my shift and I have no plans so what if I take Bea to the crèche? It's on the ground floor, and I'll wait with her while you meet with Georgina and Leo. Bea and I can chat about all things pink.'

'That's so kind of you,' Juliet said as she turned back to the lift. 'We'll have to hurry though as I have less than fifteen minutes to get to the crèche and back here for the consultation.'

Annabelle took a few long steps and pressed the down button. 'If I may make a suggestion…what if you wait here and I take Bea to the crèche so you can read over Georgina's notes? I've just refreshed everything after the ward rounds, so you can sit at the nurses' station and read up for a few minutes. I'll ask one of the nurses to take you to Room Two-Thirteen when you're ready. It would be less rushed and you'll be up to speed on the babies and mother's condition in plenty of time for the appointment.'

Juliet was so grateful the world had given her a twenty-first century Florence Nightingale but she also felt torn letting Bea go with a nurse she had known for less than five minutes. A brief internal battle prevailed, fuelled a little by Charlie's initial judging of her parenting, but common sense and her need to attend the consultation won out. 'I think Bea should be okay to go with you. She attends childcare two days a week.

'Is it all right with you, Bea, if the nurse takes you to the crèche? It's like Pennybrook back home when you go and play with the other children when Grandma and Grandpa don't have you. It's not far from here and I'll be there in about an hour once I've seen the very special patient we came all this way to help.'

'Are you going to help the lady with four babies in her tummy?'

'Yes, I am.'

'Okay, Mummy. I think you should go. Grandpa told me that you need to help the lady have the babies.'

Juliet smiled. Sometimes Bea was so wise and practical for a four-year-old. Spending quality time with her grandparents had brought an older perspective to her life and for that Juliet was grateful. She kissed the top of her daughter's head and watched her and Annabelle step closer to the opening doors of the elevator. Bea's fear, that was palpable in A&E, had all but disappeared. Annabelle did look a little similar to one of the pretty child-carers back at Pennybrook and that, Juliet surmised, went a long way to making Bea feel comfortable.

'And you can meet the other children at the crèche. They're all very nice,' Annabelle added as she reached for Bea's little hand and stepped inside the now fully open doors. 'And you can tell me about everything you have back in Australia that's pink. Do you have a pink kangaroo too?'

'No, that would be silly,' Bea said, giggling. 'But I have a pink bear and a pink....' The doors closed on Bea's chatter and Juliet felt herself smiling as she waved goodbye. Annabelle was a lovely addition to an otherwise dreadful day and she was so grateful for her assistance.

As Juliet took a moment to gather her thoughts she knew, with Bea under control, she could concentrate on the task at hand. Making sure that Charlie Warren was put in his place. She had not travelled halfway around the world, not to mention spent years qualifying in her field, to be contradicted by him without having an opportunity to deliver all of the facts. *In-utero* surgery was the quads' best hope and she would be damned if she would stand by and have Charlie convince the Abbiatis otherwise.

Juliet returned to the computer at the nurses' station and caught up with the Abbiatti quads' and their mother's observations before heading off in the direction of Georgina's room. She stood at the T-junction reading the room signs to ensure she had the right wing.

'So let's get you around to meet the parents of the infamous four,' Charlie said, startling Juliet and making her spin around. It was a voice that she would now recognise anywhere. 'I didn't want you to get lost on the way to the consult. I want the Abbiatis to hear your plan and make up their own minds. Despite what you may think, I do play fair.'

'Um…thank you,' she said with a little frown causing a furrow on her forehead. He wasn't playing fair in her books. He was on a mission and the way he looked, the way he spoke, his seemingly impeccable manners, none of it was playing fair.

He ushered her in the direction of the patient's room and she walked alongside him refusing to acknowledge to herself how he was unnerving and confusing her. Since Bea was born, Juliet felt confident in her appraisal of men and their intentions very quickly. No matter how cleverly they spun a story or expertly delivered a well-versed pick-up line. They were all the same and she knew not to trust them.

But Charlie, she had to silently admit, was the most difficult case to sum up that she had stumbled upon to date.

They walked in silence for a few steps, but as they neared the ward Charlie stopped and turned to face Juliet. 'There's something I've been wanting to say to you.'

Juliet's eyes widened and quizzically looked everywhere but at Charlie. She really didn't want to look into his eyes, not in such close proximity. Finally her gaze came back to him. His look was intense and she swallowed nervously.

'What is it?' she asked, not sure she wanted to know but equally puzzled. Even now, in his white consulting coat, he looked as dashing and irresistible as he did in his head-to-toe black leather motorcycle gear. His broad shoulders were not hidden underneath the shapeless clothing. A body like his could not be masked by anything. His boots very loudly announced bad boy even if the rest of him was temporarily dressed to indicate tame. There were definitely two sides to Charlie Warren.

'I've had time to reflect on my earlier behaviour and I wanted to apologise for jumping to a conclusion about you,' he told her.

Damn! Juliet swallowed again. How she wished with every fibre of her being she had refused the secondment and remained in Perth. Safely tucked away from what Charlie Warren could risk making her feel. It was scaring her. She had known him for less than two hours and he was confusing her more than she'd thought possible. All of her reservations and irritation about Charlie seemed to vanish, with the sound of his voice. It was a bedroom voice. Husky and innately masculine but with undertones of compassion.... and tenderness.

Why did he have to apologise? Being angry was her best line of defence. Now what would protect her from herself...and whatever she might begin to feel about Dr Charlie Warren?

CHAPTER FIVE

'GEORGIE, LEO...' CHARLIE BEGAN as Juliet entered the room carrying some handwritten notes on a clipboard along with the printed obs. 'This is Dr Juliet Turner. She is the *in-utero* surgeon who has travelled from Australia to consult on your pregnancy. She will be providing another option with regards to the condition the boys have developed. I must say upfront that I'm not supportive of this option for reasons I have already explained. However, Dr Turner has flown a long way to explain the procedure and answer your questions so I will hand over to her.' He paused and turned his attention to a very stunned Juliet. 'Dr Turner, let me introduce Leo and Georgina Abbiati.'

Juliet couldn't believe that he had just put doubt in the Abbiatis' minds before she opened her mouth. Despite his apology and consideration in ensuring she made it to the consult, he was not giving her any other professional courtesies. She stepped forward with her hand outstretched. 'Very pleased to meet you.'

Juliet knew she was up against his bias. He was stubbornly conservative and not open to accepting proven progressive procedures just as her father had suggested. It was not what she would expect at face value from the motorcycle-riding doctor. The two seemed miles apart. She drew a deep breath hoping Charlie would leave any further opinions until they were alone in his office and show a mutual professional respect and, as he said, *hand over to her*. She was not about to back away from her belief that the *in-utero* surgery was the best and most logical option for the patient. In the limited time Charlie had given her, Juliet had read the last few days' patient notes and it was exactly as she had first thought: an open and shut case in favour of laser surgery. The twin-to-twin transfusion needed to be halted immediately.

'It's a long way to come just for our babies,' Leo said as he tenderly stroked his wife's arm. 'And we appreciate it. This is a huge decision for us to make. It's our babies' lives we're talking about.'

'Of course it is and I was more than happy

to travel here so that you and your children have options to ensure for the best possible outcome,' she replied empathetically. 'The hospital board and the Assistant Head of Obstetrics believed it necessary for me to come and discuss the next management strategy that can be employed. Can you please tell me what you know about your babies' condition, so that I don't repeat anything that either Dr Warren or Mr Darrington have already covered?'

'We know that the two girls are okay and the two boys are sharing an artery or something so one of our boys is getting lots of blood and the other one not enough. Georgie's been having a special diet hoping to get all of them big enough in case they came early anyway. She's twenty-nine weeks tomorrow.'

'You certainly have an overall picture of what's happening. Twin-to-twin transfusion syndrome, or TTTS for short, is a condition of the placenta that affects identical twin pregnancies. The placenta itself is shared unequally by the twins so that one of your sons is receiving too little blood to provide the necessary nutrients to grow normally and the other too much and so his heart is being overworked. Your TTTS was diagnosed at stage three, which is already advanced, and unfortunately has progressed to stage four.' Juliet paused. She knew that she needed to be honest but what she had to say would be hard for the parents-to-be. 'I am not telling you this to add to your concerns but I need to tell it how it truly is and, while the recipient baby is coping at the moment, if we do not surgically intervene that can change quickly and he can suffer heart failure. If that happened, it would immediately cross to stage five and we cannot save him and you will only have three babies. And even then their survival will be compromised.'

The expressions on Leo's and Georgie's faces fell further. 'What do you think, Charlie?'

'I agree with Dr Turner that the boys' condition is serious but I feel the high-protein diet has assisted with the babies' gaining weight and if we continue on that path we may be able to deliver within the next two weeks if necessary.'

Juliet felt as if she were playing a polite game of medical ping-pong but she had to keep serving. 'I would like to commend Dr Warren for the exceptional care he has provided to you and your babies up to now, but unfortunately your boys' condition has worsened. I'm not convinced that without surgical intervention you'll be able to carry four healthy babies for long enough for a good outcome,' Juliet countered.

'But I don't understand why it happened,' Leo said, oblivious to the battle of medical opinion that was being waged very politely in his wife's room. 'We've asked everyone and everyone has told us we did nothing wrong, but you're the specialist. Be honest, was it something we did?'

'Not at all,' Juliet answered. 'It's something that the medical experts can't predict. The events in pregnancy that lead to TTTS are quite random events. The condition is not hereditary or genetic, nor is it caused by anything either of you did or didn't do. TTTS can literally happen to anyone having multiple births at any stage up until about thirty weeks.'

'So it's definitely not our fault?'

'Absolutely not,' Juliet responded again honestly and without hesitation.

'Charlie and Mr Darrington told us that but it's nice to hear it from you.'

Georgina's expression, on hearing confirmation about the cause of her babies' condition, was subdued but Juliet was happy that at least unwarranted guilt would not be another struggle for the quads' mother.

'We know the boys are in trouble but are there any risks to Georgie from the TTTS?' her husband asked as he looked at his wife with loving concern.

'That is something we have to consider, and another reason your wife is in Teddy's on bed rest,' Juliet continued. 'Carrying quads is in itself quite taxing on a woman's body and that stress has been increased by the TTTS. Her uterus is being stretched past what is normal for pregnancy—'

'Should you just wait then and take the babies in two weeks as Charlie says and not put Georgie at any risk?' Leo cut in.

Without giving Charlie time to interrupt, Juliet answered quickly. 'Actually no. That could've been a consideration if, since the diagnosis two days ago, the condition had not progressed, but it has and, for want of a better word, aggressively. I'm not convinced that the recipient baby would survive until thirty-one weeks. If the pregnancy was just twins, we could deliver at twenty-nine weeks. However, with quads the babies are still very small so if we can prolong the pregnancy another few weeks by having the laser surgery, the babies will be bigger when they're born and that will make their lives easier. At the moment they are all less than three pounds and we no longer have time on our side to observe their growth.'

'Like you said, Dr Turner,' Georgina responded, 'we agree that Charlie has taken such good care of me up until now we're really struggling to think about ignoring his advice. Perhaps we should have the needle and stay with bed rest.'

Charlie drew in a deep breath, plumped out his chest, and in Juliet's opinion looked like a pigeon about to mate. His polite interruptions made her believe their professional battle would lean towards a gentleman's sword fight, but a fight nonetheless, and she was right. But for the good of the mother and her babies, she would not hold back. There would be a level of professional courtesy, but she would not cower to him. Juliet was prepared to argue on the evidence-based merit of surgery and then leave the decision where it should lie. With the well-informed parents.

'While the needle you spoke of, an amniotic reduction, can work well in stage one patients, you have moved past this option very quickly. Teddy's brought me here to discuss laser surgery and the benefits and they would not have flown me halfway around the world if there was any doubt that surgery was a viable and preferable choice for you.' Juliet paused for a moment, then continued with a serious timbre in her voice. 'But I won't lie to you, there are risks in the surgical route as there are with any surgery, but the benefit far outweighs the risks. I also must let you know that if you choose to proceed with the laser surgery, then it would need to be this week. On Thursday or Friday at the latest as time is not on our side if we decide to help your sons surgically. If we leave it too long, your body will make the decision for us.'

Juliet watched Georgina's and Leo's expressions darken. It was a lot to process and, while she had not wanted to put additional pressure on either of them, she felt all the facts had to be stated. Time was unfortunately not on their side and that was the harsh realisation they all needed to accept. To deliver four living babies, something had to be done. She just prayed they chose surgery.

'Can you give us more details, like what the surgery involves and how long it will take?' Leo asked as he ceased stroking his wife's arm and reached down to hold her hand tightly.

Juliet stepped away from the bed to give the couple a little more space. Hearing news and making potential life-and-death decisions, she knew, was overwhelming and they needed to feel safe together in their own space. 'Of course,' she began and then noticed that Charlie had brought her a chair. She wasn't sure if he was being gallant and considerate or if he was trying to make her appear weary. She didn't waste time deciding which it was, instead choosing to graciously accept the chair and continue.

'The operation involves endoscopic surgery using a laser beam to cauterise the offending arteries and halt the exchange of blood between your boys. Each baby will remain connected to his primary source of blood and nutrition, the placenta, through the umbilical cord. The use of endoscopic instruments allows for short recovery time and no effect on the other babies and would be done only once during the pregnancy.'

'Dear God, we pray if we go ahead it's just one time,' Leo interrupted as he looked into his wife's tear-filled eyes. 'Georgie's been through so much over the last eighteen months with the three rounds of IVF, and that was unsuccessful, and then finding out we're having four babies conceived naturally. And now this heartbreaking news about the transfusion while I was away.'

'Leo, you're suffering as much as me, and you had to make the trip to New York,' she told him as she mopped the tears that threatened to escape. Her eyes were reddened from too many nights of crying. 'We've *both* been through so much and we're doing our best to stay strong together.'

'And we will. No matter what, we'll get through all of this. And we'll take our babies home to where they belong. Their *nonni*, all four of them, are waiting to meet their grandchildren.'

Juliet nodded. 'That's my plan and I'm so pleased to hear your positive outlook. That's exactly what your babies need.'

'Ah, you know Italians, we're a strong race and our children will be fighters too.'

'Goodness, Leo,' Georgina said. 'You sound like my father!'

'Well, it's the truth,' Charlie added. 'You and Georgie have been strong and focused since the diagnosis and that's why you should not completely rule out continuing on the current conservative path.'

Juliet swung around on her chair with a look of indignation. She could not believe what she was hearing. Charlie clearly had not *handed over to her* as he'd promised. Fuming but unable to tell Charlie how she felt, Juliet regained her composure, turned back to the couple and continued. She would let Charlie know in no uncertain terms how she felt about his interference, after the consultation. But for the moment she intended to calmly give Georgina and Leo all the information so they understood it was their choice, and theirs alone.

'Minimally invasive fetoscopic surgery is the name of the procedure and it is aptly named because it's *minimally* invasive. It involves small incisions and I will be guided by both an endoscope and sonography. Essentially it's keyhole surgery so far lower risks than open foetal surgery, which is completely opening the uterus to operate on the foetus.'

'But there's still a chance it could go wrong?' Leo asked anxiously, looking from Juliet to Charlie.

'Yes, but not undertaking the surgery has equal if not greater risk,' Juliet said honestly and, armed with further facts, she elaborated. 'I do not want you to be under the misapprehension that the safer choice is doing nothing as that is quite incorrect. In the past the twin survival rate with severe TTTS was very low, around ten per cent before ultrasound made it possible for us to make an early diagnosis and the introduction of laser surgery. I think you should consider taking advantage of this medical advance. In years gone by women had no choice but to wait and pray they did not give birth to a stillborn baby. As I have mentioned excess amniotic fluid caused by the TTTS is causing your uterus to grow to an unsustainable size. It's a condition called polyhydramnios, and it can cause premature labour.'

'I have a fifty-four-inch waist now.'

'Yes, that's a combination of four babies and the fluid and it will continue to increase,' Charlie added. 'We're monitoring that and can continue to do so, and perform the amniotic reduction procedure.'

Juliet bit her lip again. Charlie was not allowing her much space to move.

'Georgina, you will be monitored in hospital until all four babies are born, no matter your decision. However, I'm suggesting surgery because there are four very tiny babies still growing inside you and they need optimum time to grow. The final decision rests with you.'

Georgina shifted on the bed and raised her feet again. Her rounded stomach was still covered by the sheet and lightweight blanket, but only just. Her pretty face was almost hidden by the mound that held her precious babies. Juliet knew the young woman's ribs would be excruciatingly tender from the pressure of four babies.

'So you can definitely separate the blood supply?' Georgina finally asked.

'The tiny telescope in your uterus will allow me to find and destroy all the connecting vessels. This is the only treatment that can *disconnect* the twins.'

'How common is it for parents to choose laser surgery?'

'Laser surgery is now performed all over the world as more and increasing numbers of progressively attuned doctors are convinced that this will lead to the best outcomes.' Juliet's words were directed at Charlie but she did not pause over the words or look in his direction. Two could play at the same game. 'Most physicians worldwide agree that placental laser surgery results in the highest numbers of healthy survivors.'

'Including those in the UK?' Leo enquired.

'Yes, particularly in a hospital like Teddy's.'

Georgina and Leo gave each other a knowing look. 'Would I be awake?'

'Yes, Georgie, you'd be awake. You would be under conscious sedation and local anaesthetic for this procedure. We need you and the babies to be relaxed and pain free during the procedure but there's no need for a general anaesthetic.'

Leo straightened his back, took a deep resonating breath and looked at Charlie. 'Charlie, by what we're hearing, and the urgency of everything, are we right in thinking we have to make the decision tonight? It's a lot to take in and not a decision we want to make in a hurry.'

Charlie cleared his throat and stepped a little closer. 'Not quite tonight but, yes, if you choose Dr Turner's surgical option you would only have a day or two to make that decision. However, my plan would not see you making any changes other than looking at prescribing heart medication as pills given to Georgie, or injected directly into the twin if he is showing signs of heart failure. We can also look at another therapy using medication to decrease the urine output in the recipient and lessen the amount of amniotic fluid that is causing Georgie's uterus to expand.'

Juliet bit her lip. She could counter but chose not to do so. She had said enough and if they chose the non-surgical option she would remain on staff at Teddy's to help in any way she could, including the delivery. But she hoped they would choose her way forward and she would be able to use her surgical skills to increase the babies' chances of survival and happy and healthy lives.

Georgina and Leo looked at each other with what Juliet knew would feel like the weight of the world on their shoulders but their love for each other still shone brightly in their eyes. Finally Leo spoke. 'Is it all right if we sleep on it?'

'Of course,' Charlie and Juliet said in unison then they too looked at each other. But it was not lovingly; their look was more of an aloof stare.

Juliet had felt as if she were on a roller coaster since she'd touched down at Heathrow, and even before that with the last-minute packing. But now it was a different type of roller coaster. The emotional type. And for which she had not willingly purchased a ticket, nor even had any idea she would be experiencing. But in the few hours since Charlie had stepped into her life and lifted her tiny daughter into his arms, she had ridden highs and lows that she'd never imagined. He was opinionated and brash; considerate and caring; her old school colleague and stubborn opponent; and still, to her annoyance, attractive.

He was quite the package and she definitely didn't want to peel back too many layers or get too close. Charlie was confusing her and, working together for the next few weeks, she wondered how successfully she could avoid getting to know more about him. A conservative, bad-boy biker with attitude who seemed to adore children, or at least her child. Could he be any more complex? She doubted it.

And she wasn't convinced she wanted to understand Charlie Warren.

CHAPTER SIX

WITH LEO AND GEORGINA left alone to think everything over, Juliet had a chance to meet the rest of Teddy's nursing staff. Although Juliet had seen the Royal Cheltenham hospital emergency department up close and personal with Bea, Charlie knew that she had not seen Teddy's properly, so he took it upon himself to offer to show her around the centre dedicated to babies and birth. But not before setting the parameters of the working relationship in his mind.

'I think you would have to agree that we both behaved quite poorly in there,' he began, thinking that they should get everything out in the open and start afresh. 'Fortunately not that Georgina or Leo noticed.'

'I'm sorry, are you questioning *my* behaviour?'

'I'm just saying that we could have handled things a little more diplomatically.'

'So you're saying that we *both* behaved poorly and *we* could have handled things better?'

Charlie frowned. 'Yes, as I also said, it was done in a very polite manner so that the Abbiatis did not sense any professional tension, but you have to admit we were walking a fine line.'

Juliet's hands suddenly took pride of place on her hips as she began pacing, then drew to a halt in front of him. 'I can't believe what you're saying and I refuse to accept culpability for your, as you Englishmen say, *poor form*. I was seconded over here and you were clearly the one stirring doubt, if not confusion.'

Charlie studied Juliet's face. Even angry, she was very beautiful. And Juliet was clearly angry. She was riled up and ready to pounce on him for even suggesting that she had participated in the battle of wills. It was apparent when challenged Juliet was like a cat with an arched back. He wondered what made her so defensive. Had she been on the receiving end of too many challenges over her career? Or was it more than that? Was her attitude of fight or flight born from something outside work?

He suddenly stopped his line of thought mid-journey. What she did or did not do outside work was not his business. Whatever had caused, or was still causing, Juliet to fight back was not his concern. She was a grown woman, who had no doubt endured some heartache and some of life's lessons, but that did not excuse her from professional scrutiny.

Charlie eyed Juliet again. In fact he had barely taken his eyes away from her. All five feet four inches. But despite her petite appearance, he had quickly learnt that she was no shrinking violet. And he doubted she would tolerate fools either. He quickly realised that he wasn't about to win the argument. And suddenly, to his surprise, he was willing to accept the decision was where it needed to be, with the parents of the babies at risk. They had been given the facts. He couldn't do any more.

'Fair call, Dr Turner,' he offered. 'I'm sorry for the start we've had. Shall we begin again? Let's put the consultation behind us. One way or the other it looks as if we'll be spending time together so we should try and make this work.'

Charlie wasn't sure what had motivated him to call a professional truce but it seemed the right thing to do. He hoped she knew his words were genuine. He was calling a cease-fire. It was a masculine apology but sincere nonetheless. And one he hoped that she would accept.

She extended her hand. 'Truce accepted, Dr Warren. Let's agree to disagree and allow the Abbiatis to decide without further interference.'

As he met her handshake the warmth of her skin against his almost made him recant the apology so they could return to adversaries. He pulled his hand free as soon as he was able.

'We're both clearly passionate about what we do and that's a great thing so we will just have to respect our differing opinions and work alongside each other as best we can,' he said.

'Yes, and one of us will clearly be pleased with their decision and the other disappointed but we will simply wear it,' she added.

Charlie said nothing for a moment as he looked at the tiny powerhouse standing near him. She was without doubt one of the best in her field, and, despite not agreeing with that particular obstetric intervention, he had immeasurable respect for her skills. Her reputation had preceded her. But there was something other than respect simmering below the surface for him and it was making him uncomfortable. Very uncomfortable.

He walked in the direction of the large digital directory board in Reception. 'It might be a good idea if you took a look around and familiarised yourself with Teddy's. It would be best if you met everyone and knew where everything was in case you're needed.'

'You mean for *when* I'm needed?' she responded.

'Let's wait and see.'

The introductions soon became an induction. As she met each of the medical staff she learnt about the layout and workings of Teddy's. The nursing staff gave Juliet a message from Annabelle, letting her know that Bea had settled in well and that she was enjoying a light lunch with the other children while listening to a story. Knowing that, Juliet decided to keep on the tour and learn as much as she could about the hospital.

The reputation of Teddy's had been a driving force in Juliet's accepting the secondment. The opportunity to consult and operate in a hospital with facilities second to none in all of Europe was too good to refuse.

Juliet thanked Charlie for showing her the ropes.

'Not at all. It's been an eventful start for you and I hope Bea will be all right tonight. I know I don't have to mention it, but just give her a little oral analgesia if she has trouble sleeping and she should be fine by tomorrow.'

'I will.'

As Charlie watched Juliet walk away he realised that he hadn't wanted the tour to end. He had enjoyed his time with Juliet. She was challenging him and he felt the closest to alive that he had in a long time. They came from polar opposites. Both geographically and professionally. She was forging new ground surgically and he was of the belief that monitoring with minimal surgical intervention was the better method. But despite their differences, he admired her courage.

He had been an OBGYN for many years, and his conservative approach had always provided great outcomes for the mothers and the babies. Although as he walked back to his office he admitted to himself that he had not dealt with the complication of TTTS in quadruplets. As he sat down behind his desk, to stretch his legs out and read his emails before another ward round, he conceded they were on an even playing field with regard to experience. Neither had a track record that could negate the other. So neither one of them could say with any evidence that their treatment plan was better. It was purely subjective and tainted by preference.

Juliet for taking risks.

Charlie for avoiding them every day since he had taken a chance on the icy road and lost.

Juliet and a very tired Bea arrived back at their hotel late in the afternoon. Bea had enjoyed her time at the crèche and was not in a hurry to leave. Juliet suspected it was due to the fuss that Annabelle and the children had made of her. After lunch and the story, her mind had been distracted from the traumatic start to the day by the children all wanting to draw pictures on her cast and ask questions about koalas and kangaroos. She'd been the centre of attention and she'd managed that role well. When Juliet had popped up to collect her, she'd looked through the large glass window that was decorated with paper cutouts of snowflakes to see Bea happily playing with the other children. Juliet had been convinced earlier in the day that bringing her daughter on the trip was a terrible idea, but as she'd witnessed her smiling and happily playing despite the cast the idea had left terrible territory.

A classic Georgian property, not too far from the hospital, had been restored and refurbished as an exclusive, eleven-room boutique hotel and it would be their accommodation for a day or so until Juliet could source something more practical for the two of them. Their room was toasty warm with a large bed covered in far too many oversized pillows and the softest mattress. The warmth was created by an antique radiator and the all-white decor, complete with heavy damask drapes and matching bedspread, was elegance in abundance. She felt very spoilt as the hospital board had insisted on covering the cost of the expensive room until she secured something else, in addition to her business-class flight and that of her daughter.

Back in Perth, she lived in a small home not too far from her parents and equally close to the hospital and Pennybrook childcare centre. When she'd purchased the three-bedroom house, it had been a very practical decision. It was a nice house but not ostentatious. Understated in its exterior appearance and equally in the interior. Juliet wasn't in love with her home but the location meant she could drop off Bea and collect her easily from childcare or her grandparents' home. Most decisions after Bea was born were practical. And never rushed. Up until this trip, Juliet had considered and reconsidered every move she made. Although Charlie clearly thought she was a risk-taker in suggesting the surgical intervention, she thought just the opposite. She carefully weighed up the risks, and never blindly jumped into anything. She had learnt the hard way by rushing into a relationship with Bea's father and she never planned on doing that again.

In fact, she swore on it.

The ambience of their hotel room was something Juliet loved almost immediately, along with the breathtaking scenery of the Cotswolds. It surprised Juliet that, while she had worried she would feel out of place, she quickly felt comfortable in the South Midlands of England. She was a long way from home but she didn't feel entirely lost.

As they sat at the small mahogany card table that doubled as a dining table for two, eating their room-service dinner of a hearty beef stew and finished off with a homemade apple pie, Juliet felt as if she had been transported back to another time. Bea managed to eat her children's size serving even with her sling in place and Juliet felt sure she would sleep well with a full tummy.

But no matter how stunning the room, Juliet had to admit the gorgeous antique bath positioned by the large bay window was completely impractical for a four-year-old with a cast. She felt so sorry for her tiny daughter as she stood her next to the porcelain wash basin and used the fluffy white washcloths to give her a freshen up. It would have been too awkward to place Bea into the free-standing and very deep bath. She needed to check the bathroom of the longer-term accommodation before she signed anything, she thought as she dried Bea and slipped her into snuggly warm pyjamas. Fortunately the pyjama top was made of a stretch knit and quite loose fitting so she could slip it over the cast. But working around her daughter's broken arm was not how she'd seen the first day ending.

With Bea snuggled in bed after some pain relief and drifting off to sleep, Juliet ran a bath for herself.

'Mummy,' Bea called out sleepily across the warm room.

'Yes, sweetie, what is it?' Juliet asked as she took a nightdress out of her suitcase, which was open and lying alongside Bea's. Juliet decided there was no point unpacking and using the ample white built-in wardrobe, which blended into the wall colour, or the ornately carved chest of drawers. They wouldn't be staying long enough.

'Why duth Grandpa call you honey and not Juliet?'

'He's just always called me honey since I was a little girl.'

'Ith that becauth he'th your daddy?'

'I guess so. It's his special name for me because I'm his daughter and everyone else calls me Juliet.'

'Charlie called me honey...'

Juliet stopped what she was doing. 'When?' she asked with a puzzled look.

'When I fell in the playground and he picked me up. Duth that mean Charlie could be my daddy?'

Juliet felt her stomach fall and her heart race as she dropped closed her suitcase. Her fallen stomach was the reaction to the unexpected daddy question and just thinking of Charlie in the role of Bea's father made her heart race. She swallowed a lump that had risen in her throat. Charlie's handsome face appeared in her mind. She no longer pictured Bea's father or even thought of him when she looked at Bea.

But now she suddenly pictured Charlie.

With legs shaking, Juliet walked back to her daughter and sat beside her, stroking her face and watching her tired eyes struggle to stay open. They were slowly closing as she kissed her gently. Juliet was trying to find the words to answer Bea. She was still too young to understand what had really happened and why she didn't have a daddy.

'No, my sweet, Charlie is not your daddy. But one day when you're much bigger we can talk about your daddy.' With that she pulled up the covers over her daughter.

'Okay.'

'Sweet dreams.'

As Juliet tiptoed back to the bath she heard her daughter mumble, 'Mummy?'

'Yes, sweetie.'

'I think Charlie would make a nice daddy.'

Juliet felt momentarily overwhelmed. It was obvious now that her daughter missed having a father. With a heavy heart, Juliet removed the last of her clothing in the soft light of the bedside lamp and climbed into the steaming bubbles, where she remained for a good half an hour thinking about her life and about Bea's. Her daughter's question was spinning along with all the others she had for herself. Her mind was on overload and Bea's innocent curiosity added another weight.

While the travel was beginning to take its toll, the question of Bea's paternity was now an issue and one that she had no idea how exactly she would answer. Soon she would want more answers. And Juliet would have to answer each and every question as honestly as she could without letting her know that her father was a cad.

Juliet's eyes felt heavier and heavier as she reached for an oversized towel and stepped carefully from the bath. She was exhausted. Mentally and physically. It had been a whirlwind since she'd stepped off the final plane at Heathrow. Then she admitted silently the whirlwind had begun before she and Bea had even boarded the first aircraft. The push to hand over her patients at the Perth Women's and Children's Medical Centre in a matter of hours and packing their suitcases in temperatures hovering around one hundred degrees for freezing cold weather and all the while questioning the practicalities of travelling with a four-year-old. As she dried herself and slipped the nightdress over her head she heard the soft breathing of her sleeping daughter and knew that no matter what happened or what they faced they would do it together. And they would be just fine.

Barefoot, she tiptoed over to her side of the

bed, slipped in between the brushed cotton sheets, turned down her mobile phone and turned off the bedside light. Sleep overtook her the moment her head rested on the softness of the duck-down pillows.

'Mummy, wake up! Someone'th here,' the lispy voice announced.

Juliet opened her eyes to see Bea standing beside the bed and looking in the direction of the hotel-room door. There was firm and unrelenting knocking. Not brash but loud enough to seem urgent. Juliet climbed from her bed, kissed the top of her daughter's head and grabbed her robe from the end of the bed where she had dropped it the night before.

'Who is it?'

'Charlie Warren,' came the response, but even without his self-identification his voice told her immediately that it was him.

Juliet's brow knitted. What on earth was he doing at her door? The heavy drapes stopped her seeing how dark or light it was outside but she imagined it was early; she felt as if she had barely been asleep.

'Is there something wrong? Has Georgina progressed to stage five?'

'No. Georgina's stable but they've made

their decision and I thought I'd let you know first-hand.'

Juliet crossed to the door, running her fingers through the messy curls. She didn't care at that moment about her appearance. She just hoped the news was good and they had chosen surgery. She opened the door ready to ask that question when she came face to face with a vision head to toe in black leather. Suddenly she felt senses that had lain dormant for many years awaken without warning. Charlie stood before her, once again dressed in his leather riding gear, and holding his helmet in his leather-gloved hand. The same hand that had so tenderly applied Bea's cast the day before. This was the man that called Bea *honey* and made her think he might be her father. The look was intoxicating and took her breath and words away but allowing him into her life scared her too.

'Are you okay?'

'Yes,' she finally managed. 'You startled me. I was still asleep. I'm as keen as you to know the answer but it's still so early. Did the Abbiatis call you in the middle of the night?'

'No,' he replied. 'They spoke to me on my nine o'clock rounds.'

'Nine o'clock rounds?' she asked incredulously.

'I called your phone but it went straight to message bank and you didn't call back so here I am.'

'I never heard your call,' she told him with a slight frown. 'What time is it now?'

Charlie looked at his watch. 'Nearly ten-thirty.'

'Really? That means we slept for twelve hours.'

'I've been watching TV, Mummy.'

Juliet looked down at her daughter, who had cleverly managed to slip on her sling, and then turn on the cartoon channel on the television.

'I can't believe I slept in that long. You must be hungry, darling.'

'A little.'

Charlie smiled. Bea was adorable and he was beginning to feel that there might be a slim chance Juliet might be just as lovely if he got to know her better. He admired the fact she told him exactly how she felt. She didn't tiptoe around him like everyone else who *felt sorry for the widower*. He could see it in their faces and hear it in their voices. He had attended the hospital fundraiser in the hope the staff would see him as something other than a recluse. Charlie liked that Juliet was unaware of his wife's death and he assumed that was why she was able to stand up to him. She was the first person to do that in two years. Being around her made him realise he missed being challenged and being held accountable.

And her conviction in her treatment plan for Georgina Abbiati made him feel slightly less concerned about the surgical intervention although he still did not agree.

'What if I take you two ladies out for brunch?' He wanted to spend more time with the beautiful woman with the messy hair and the gorgeous smile who was still dressed in her robe. He couldn't explain it to himself—it was as if he had known Juliet and Bea for more than one day. His attraction was more than skin deep and it defied logic and his promise to himself that he would never get involved with anyone. But standing so close to Juliet, he felt that promise fading and the desire to know her increasing.

'Is this a brunch to break good news or bad?' she asked without a smile. 'Are you here to brag of your victory and tell me that the Abbiatis have chosen your conservative treatment option? Is that the reason you've come in person?'

Charlie was taken aback. He had not seen that reaction coming. His agenda had been very different. He just felt a pull to be with

Juliet, to learn more about her away from the hospital, and against his better judgement he had decided to act upon it. Now he knew that was a stupid idea. Reckless in fact. He barely knew Juliet and, for some ridiculous reason, he wanted to spend his free time with her. And with Bea. Suddenly he was grateful she had given him the perspective he needed. He had no business being at her hotel. He should have left a message and waited until she had arrived at the hospital. He was better off alone.

It was the way he liked it.

And the way it should be.

'You're right, it was a bad idea,' he said as he stepped back and opened the hotel-room door. 'I'll leave you ladies to enjoy your late breakfast alone. And by the way, Juliet, the Abbiatis decided on the fetoscopic placental laser surgery. I guess I was just the gracious loser in a professional differing of opinion… offering to share a meal.'

With that he closed the door on Juliet.

And to stirrings he knew he had no right to act upon.

CHAPTER SEVEN

'CHARLIE, PLEASE WAIT,' Juliet called down the passageway. She couldn't follow him dressed in only her robe. 'I'm sorry, I was rude and ungracious.'

Charlie stopped long enough to turn and see her in the doorway. Her messy hair, the spattering of freckles across the bridge of her nose, and her pretty amber eyes that looked genuinely remorseful. He was grateful that she had sent him walking. It was for the best. She was too close to exactly what he didn't have room for in his life. And definitely didn't deserve. A pretty, intelligent woman with a fighting spirit. And a daughter who was cute as a button.

'Apology accepted. I'll see you at the hospital later, then. I've an opening at one-thirty if you would like to meet. We need to schedule in the surgery, brief the theatre team and then book another pre-op consultation as soon as possible.'

His tone was brusque and he didn't wait for a reply as Juliet watched him disappear out of sight. She closed her bedroom door and raced to the window with Bea in tow. Pulling back the heavy damask curtains to see him emerge from the building and climb onto the shiny black bike that he had parked in the small guest car park. He pulled down his helmet, and turned his head. Nervously she dropped the curtains before he saw her watching him. It appeared Dr Charlie Warren, intentionally or unintentionally, was going to make her second day in the Cotswolds as confusing as the first.

Charlie rode away but not before he noticed Juliet looking from her window. He saw in his rear-view mirror that she had closed the curtains as quickly as she had opened them. While he had accepted her apology he couldn't help but wonder as he headed along the leafy streets on his way to Teddy's what had made the Australian specialist so quickly think the worst of him.

Admittedly, the previous day he had been the one to jump to conclusions, and perhaps had not been his professional best at the consultation, but he had apologised for both. And to make amends and let her know that he would not challenge the Abbiatis' decision he had driven over to tell her in person. But once he'd known that neither Bea nor Juliet had eaten, it had felt natural to offer a shared brunch.

As he rounded the next corner, he told himself that it was his olive branch. But there was more to it and, as he righted himself on the large motorbike before the next curve, he silently accepted that Juliet had broken through his tough exterior shell. She had made him think of more than work. More than the mothers and the babies and the families he was helping to create. In twenty-four hours she and Bea had reminded him of all those things he'd wanted and dreamed of before the accident. Before the loss of his wife made him lose hope in the future.

But her reaction to his reaching out was unexpected. Shooting him down by questioning his motives.

Was it jet lag or was Juliet Turner always on the defensive? He wasn't sure but, with his hand on the throttle, he rode a little faster than usual. Although Charlie had grown up in the stunning Cotswolds countryside, he appreciated the architecture and landscape that defined the part of England he called home, but not that day. Instead of noticing the Regency town houses and their intricate ironwork balconies and painted stucco façades or the rolling green hills that were blanketed in pristine snow, he could only picture Juliet's face as he travelled back to work. Equally confused about what made Juliet so quick to judge...and what had really driven him to deliver the news in person.

Juliet knocked on the door. The brass plate read Dr Charlie Warren, OBGYN. She was in the right place.

'Come in.'

Juliet opened the door and entered with mixed emotions. She was thrilled that the surgery would take place and the quads would in her opinion have the best chance of survival, but her behaviour at the hotel a few hours earlier still bothered her. And underneath she knew that was because Charlie Warren was affecting her and she was confused and scared.

But despite those feelings unnerving her, the fact the obstinate but handsome OBGYN had reached out to her made her feel a little special. Perhaps that was why she took extra time to choose her outfit. A long black knitted dress that hugged her slim hips. It had a roll collar and she had added a silver necklace and a black patent boot with a medium height heel. It was her smart apology outfit, she told herself. The previous day's travelling clothes were for comfort and that morning he had seen her in her pyjamas so she wanted to show a level of professionalism in her dressing. There was no other reason for her to wear the figure-hugging dress.

The tight knit also kept her warm. Cheltenham was a cold place. That was all.

How could there be any other reason? It certainly wasn't to impress Charlie Warren the man.

'Hello, Juliet. Please take a seat. I won't be a moment. I'm just emailing through a medical report to a GP in London.'

'Thank you,' she said as she sat in the chair opposite him.

Juliet took the time to let her gaze wander around the office. But there was nothing telling about any of it. No personal belongings that jumped out and showed her a little about Charlie. No photos, just a couple of certificates that provided evidence of his qualifications. Without appearing nosey, she searched from her vantage point for something that would let her know more about him. There was nothing. No hint. It appeared that Dr Warren had no life outside his work...or if he did he was hiding it.

'I have taken the liberty of booking the operating theatre,' he began as he turned his attention to Juliet. 'And also confirming with the Abbiatis that the surgery will be on Friday.'

'Thank you.'

'Don't thank me, I'm just extending a professional courtesy on behalf of the board.'

Juliet frowned. His change in demeanour was extraordinary. But she knew she had been the cause. Her earlier reaction was cold and dismissive and just plain rude.

'Juliet, don't misread my actions for a change of mind. It isn't. I still don't think that surgery is the best option and, while I will not raise the issue again with the parents as they have made their decision, I still have grave concerns.'

'Well, I'm grateful that we can agree at least to provide a united front even if behind the scenes there is still a great divide.'

Juliet noticed a flick in his jaw. Finely covered with dark blond shadow, it was defined but tense.

'A very great divide.'

'May I ask why?'

'Because I know you have experience in TTTS and this procedure, your papers prove it, but you have never, according to my research, undertaken this with quads.'

'I have with triplets,' she argued.

'Once,' he returned. 'I read your notes.'

'Yes, once, but successfully and I am not operating on all four. Only two of the four are involved.'

'That's where you're wrong. You're exposing all four to a risk.'

'I agree but the benefits outweigh the risk—'

'I don't agree with that rationale. You're risking all four babies to save one and even success with that foetus is not guaranteed. It could take up to a month after the baby is born to know if there are any residual effects from the surgery. And even a year later in some cases long-term side effects have been diagnosed.'

'But the child may not live at all if we don't proceed.' Juliet slumped a little in her chair. Her apology meeting was turning sour quickly. Charlie's defensive stance was back again. She hoped she would have been more gracious if she had been the one assisting him with his treatment plan instead of the other way around. But she accepted that was easier said as the victor and her reaction a few hours earlier, suspecting he was delivering bad news, didn't show any sign of gracious defeat. Perhaps they were alike after all. But she would never know because she was the one who had won this battle.

'I've been performing this procedure for many years and before proceeding the Abbiatis will be fully informed of the risk.'

'One additional baby complicates things ten-fold and I'm not sure that you'll be experienced enough to deal with those complications should they arise.'

Juliet decided to stand and signal the end of the meeting. It was going nowhere and it was pointless in her opinion. 'I don't see any value in going around in circles. The parents have agreed, Teddy's board flew me over and the theatre is booked thanks to you. It would appear the surgery is a fait accompli.'

'If it's not successful, I'll be noting my objections in a report to the board.'

'I would expect no less,' she replied as she crossed to the door. 'Will I have an office during my secondment? I think it would be a good idea so that I can have some time to look over the reports privately.' Her eyebrow was raised as she looked directly at Charlie. She hoped it was a look that didn't leave room for questions or second-guessing. It was a demand not a polite request that he could choose whether to approve. He had taken it back to adversarial colleagues. They were right back to where they started.

'I'll see what we can do.'

'Now that's settled, I'll be back tomorrow with my laptop ready to log on and begin the pre-op preparations.'

Juliet chatted with the nurses and asked to meet the midwife who was looking after Georgina.

'That's Ella O'Brien,' Annabelle offered. 'She's not on today but will be back tomorrow.'

Juliet thanked her and then left to visit Georgina.

'Leo's just gone home to get me some fresh clothes. I guess you heard we're going ahead with the surgery.'

'I did, and I must say I'm very pleased. I truly believe it's the best option.'

'So do we,' Georgina said with nerves and a little doubt still evident in her voice. 'We really like Charlie but we got to thinking if the board has flown you all the way here then they must believe in the surgery too. We didn't think they would go to that much trouble and expense if it wasn't something they believe worthwhile. We just don't know why Charlie doesn't feel the same way as them.'

'Dr Warren is a great doctor, and he has every right to have a different opinion. Medicine can be quite subjective at times and sometimes doctors differ but they both want the best for the patient. Dr Warren's taken the very best care of you up to now but the board do agree that the laser surgery will give you the best chance of taking four babies home with you.'

'We pray every day for them all. We've named them, you know.'

'That's wonderful. Are the names a secret?'

'We have told our family and Charlie, Ella and Mr Darrington. We like Graham and Rupert for the boys and Lily and Rose for the girls.'

'I feel very honoured to know, and they are the loveliest names,' Juliet said sincerely. She thought they were such sweet, old-fashioned names but they didn't sound very southern European at all.

'I guess you're wondering why they sound so English and not Italian.'

'You're a mind reader.'

'Not really, I think we're going to be asked that a lot but our families moved here from

Italy many years ago. Leo and I mct at Italian school so traditions are important but since we both come from huge families, I have five siblings and Leo has eight brothers and sisters, so the grandparents all have grandchildren named after them, and more than a few cousins share names too. We wanted our babies to be different. It's not that we don't love our culture, it's just we want them to have their own identity, which will be difficult enough with two sets of identical twins, let alone if they share names with their cousins. So we have our parents' blessings to give them very special names.'

'Were you born here, or in Italy?'

'Leo and I were both born in London. Leo's grandparents did very well producing rice and maize in the region of Abbiategrasso, in Lombardy in Italy, and that's where his surname originated. They sent his father to London for an education with the hopes he would return to his home, but instead he graduated from law, met a beautiful young Italian woman, married and settled in London raising Leo and his brothers and sisters. My grandparents' background was in grapes and olives in Umbria. My father was also sent to London for higher education and along with his international commerce degree came an English bride, my mother, who loved all things Italian including my father. And soon,' she said, looking down at her oversized belly, 'there will be another instant generation of Abbiatis a long way from Italy.'

'Well, I think the names are just gorgeous and I'm sure the children will make you very proud as they grow up.'

'So you're privy to the babies' names too?' came a deep and now familiar voice from the doorway. 'Well, I must say you've become a member of the Abbiati family more quickly than I did. It took me the best part of a month before that information was entrusted to me.'

Juliet turned to see Charlie in the doorway to the private hospital room.

'I feel quite special at this moment.'

'And so you should, for you know the names of the children you have been given the opportunity to save.'

Juliet suddenly felt the weight of the Abbiatis' decision fall squarely on her shoulders. She swallowed hard, unsure if unsettling her was Charlie's intention. If so he had succeeded.

'I will have a great surgical team, experienced—'

'And ready for the unexpected,' Charlie cut in.

Juliet was not impressed. She had hoped his doubts would not be voiced any more but apparently that was not the case. At least she was pleased his delivery was subtle enough not to cause any concern to Georgina. She was still unaware of the professional rivalry. For that Juliet was grateful.

'I would expect no less from any team, primed for success and prepared for the unexpected, but in this case I doubt there will be any surprises. We know there are four babies, and we know there's one problem to solve and then bed rest for you for another few weeks until they are all healthy and a good size for delivery. And on that note, Dr Warren and I need to discuss the procedure and have a scheduled meeting now.'

'We do?'

'We do.'

'Then, Georgie, I will see you later,' Charlie said as he followed Juliet from the room. Once they were out of earshot, Juliet did not hold back.

'You promised you would not try to unsettle my patient. She has made her decision and there is no point in you questioning them now.'

'Your patient? Georgina is my patient and

has been for nineteen weeks since the quads were identified.'

'Well, she'll be your former patient unless you promise to cease this interference.'

'Since when does advice to my patient constitute interference?' he asked as he headed in the direction of his office.

'From where I'm standing that's exactly what it is and I won't stand for it. So please back off or I'll be forced to go to Oliver Darrington and ask to have you removed if he wants me to stay.' Juliet kept up with his fast pace.

'Is that a threat?'

'I'm not sure… I guess if you don't accept your behaviour to be tantamount to undue interference then I really don't have to acknowledge whether mine is a threat.'

'I said in front of Georgina that you have the opportunity to save her babies. They chose your procedure. It's now in your hands. A fact. And as for the team expecting the unexpected, that is my way of saying they are experienced and the Abbiatis have nothing to worry about. My words were designed to bring comfort to the quads' mother and by the look on her face they did just that. Did she look panicked?'

Juliet considered his words and began

to think she might have overreacted again. 'Well, no.'

'That's because I know my patient, I've been treating her for almost three months now and I have built a good rapport with her.' He stopped outside his office.

At that moment, an orderly appeared wheeling a trolley laden with boxes. 'This is the last of the archived records, Dr Warren. A desk is being brought up from storage along with a chair and a sofa. Oh, and I've asked the cleaning crew to freshen up the office next door for the Aussie doctor as you requested and the flowers you ordered will be here first thing tomorrow. I'm sorry the office wasn't cleaned up this morning when you asked but we've been flat out. I wasn't sure if she'd arrived yet but it will be all done by lunchtime.'

'I guess your office will be ready for you to move in tomorrow, then, Juliet,' Charlie said as he left Juliet alone with another onslaught of thoughts.

Each one of them making her feel smaller by the minute. She had once again misjudged Charlie and in the process demanded something he had already planned on providing. Before he graciously asked her out to brunch to give her the good news. Suddenly she thought the ogre's shoes were more befitting her feet.

Juliet collected Bea without trying to find Charlie and offering to thank him. He had already organised an office for her before she'd made the demand earlier in the day. She felt foolish and thought better than trying to make amends yet again. She had made a habit of offending him that day just as he had of offending her the day before. He had made an effort to be courteous but the orderlies hadn't been able to deliver. The fact she did not have an office was not his fault.

And the flowers he ordered? What on earth did that mean? After the disastrous start to the day, and the terrible ending, he still wanted to make her feel at home with flowers. This man was more of a riddle by the minute. Just when she thought she had worked him out, he surprised her. Only this time it was a nice surprise and an extremely humbling one for Juliet.

Somehow she would make amends. But exactly how would take some time to figure out.

'Mummy!' came the little voice. 'I have a friend. Her name's Emma.' A little girl with flaming red hair and a toothy grin was holding Bea's hand. 'We played yesterday. And we played today. She'th such a good drawer. Her mummy'th a doctor too.'

'Hello, Emma.'

'Hello,' the little girl replied in the softest voice.

'Can Emma come home and play?'

'That would be lovely one day if her mummy says yes, but just not today, Bea, because we have to find another place to live. Somewhere with a nice bath and your own room.'

Bea studied her mother's face for a minute. 'Okay, Mummy,' she finally said with a smile. 'Bye Emma. See you tomorrow.'

'Bye, Bea,' the little girl replied before she ran back to the toys on the play mat in the centre of the room.

Juliet popped her daughter's woollen cape over her shoulders and led her to the car they had hired that morning. She was happy that Bea had made a new friend so quickly. She definitely had much better social skills than her mother, Juliet thought.

'I've found two houses that might be nice so we might just pop in and see them. A man with the keys is meeting us at the first one in half an hour. We can't stay in the hotel because it doesn't give us much room and the bath just won't do. It might be nice to have your own room—perhaps one day this week Emma might come over and play.'

'I hope so,' Bea said as she looked out of the window at the buildings as they drove down the main street of the town.

Juliet suddenly spotted a quaint tea room. 'Would you like something to eat?'

'Yeth, please.'

'Let's see if this little restaurant has Devonshire cream tea,' she said as she checked her rear-vision mirror, then pulled the car over and parked.

'What'th that, Mummy?'

'Scones and jam and cream.'

'Yummy!'

Almost an hour later and quite full on the fluffy scones, homemade raspberry jam and freshly whipped cream, Juliet and Bea arrived at the first house. It was a fully furnished cottage only ten minutes from Teddy's. She pulled her small sedan into the lane beside the house, unsure of where else to park, and walked briskly around to the front gate. The lettings agent was already there. He looked about sixty years of age with a happy face with a ruddy complexion, strawberry-blond hair and wearing a tweed coat and a scarf.

'Good afternoon, Dr Turner. I'm Eugene Parry.'

'Hello, Eugene,' Juliet said as she approached him with her hand extended. 'Please call me Juliet.'

'Certainly, Juliet,' the man said as he unlocked the front door of the thatched-roof cottage. 'It's a lovely little place, this one. Just came back on the market for renting a week ago after the temporary bank manager left. They found a local to fill the role so the other one headed back to London leaving this vacant and you can have it on a monthly basis. No need for a long-term contract.'

Juliet stepped inside and was immediately taken by how cosy the home felt. It was small but very pretty inside.

'Two bedrooms, as I said, and an eat-in kitchen along with this sitting room,' Eugene said as they stood in the middle of the carpeted room. It was a little cold but Juliet knew with the flick of a switch the heating would change that quickly. 'There's a lovely garden room out the back, which is delightful in summer but not so nice in the chilly weather. Oh, and there's a bath and shower in the newly renovated bathroom.'

Juliet was happy to hear those words and took Bea by the hand to look around. The pretty tastefully wallpapered sitting room more than met her requirements with a large floral sofa and a big leather armchair, a coffee table and a large television. The master bedroom was very simply decorated in tones of blue, with a queen-sized bed and attractive blue-and-cream-striped curtains and a cream damask quilt cover. A free-standing dark wood wardrobe took up one corner of the room and the other corner held a matching large dresser with an oval mirror.

'Where'th my room?'

'Let's go and find out.'

And they did. And it was just perfect. It was painted in tones of peach and there were two twin single beds and a white dresser and robe. The curtains were peach floral with yellow window ties. And there was a four-foot fluffy yellow rabbit sitting under the window beside a toy box.

'The owners have two granddaughters and they used to come and stay but now they're all grown up so they've left it here for others to enjoy.'

'I like it, Mummy.'

'I like it too. We'll take it.'

Aware that the next few days would be hectic leading up to the surgery, Juliet decided, once she had signed the rental agreement, to leave the hotel and move into the cottage immediately. The estate agent was happy as the hospital provided a reference and a guarantee. So Juliet was approved instantly. He had given her the keys and explained how the heater and the stove worked and left.

'Well, Bea, it looks like we have our own little home for the next few weeks. I've rented it for a month so we can stay here for Christmas and New Year's Eve.'

'Do we have milk and biscuits?'

Juliet smiled at Bea's funny random question and the look of worry on her daughter's face. 'We will get some milk and biscuits and a few other things. In fact, we should go now and stock the pantry before the shops close.'

Together they locked up, hopped back into the car and headed off to fill the cupboards and refrigerator with all they would need.

And as she drove into town Juliet realised she was no longer anxious about being so far from home. Despite her topsy-turvy relationship with Charlie Warren she was suddenly feeling quite at home in the Cotswolds.

Without warning she began to question if in fact it was because of him that she was feeling so at home.

CHAPTER EIGHT

IT WAS FIVE o'clock in the afternoon when they returned. Bea was napping on the sofa, with the heater warming the house, and dinner for two was cooking in the oven. Juliet had bought half a dozen small pork chops and decided to roast them with root vegetables. She thought they could have leftovers the next night. The house was quiet and the delicious aroma of the cooking made her think of home. She looked at her watch and did the mental arithmetic and quickly realised it was one in the morning back home. While she knew her parents loved her, one a.m. was not the time to test the depth of those feelings. She would wait until morning. She had called from the airport to tell them she was safe and since then they had each sent texts. There was nothing else to report. Nothing had happened. They hadn't really met anyone. As she put her feet up on the ottoman and leant back into the softness of the cushions, she realised that technically wasn't correct. Bea had met her new best friend, Emma.

And Juliet had met Charlie. Complicated, handsome, argumentative Charlie. She closed her eyes for a moment.

Who was he really?

And why was he making her think about him when he wasn't around? For almost five years, she had not given a man another romantic thought, until now.

Dinner was lovely and they both ate well, then Juliet washed the dishes before she gave Bea a nice warm bath, paying particular care to keep her cast dry. As she wrapped her daughter in a fluffy bath sheet before slipping her into her pyjamas, Juliet smiled at the little girl and thought how strong she had been. She couldn't have been more proud of her daughter. She didn't fuss or complain about it at all. Bea just worked around the cast and made the best of it. She was indeed a very special little girl. Despite having her own room, and thinking it was very pretty, that night she decided to sleep with her mother in the big bed. And after her favourite story, they both fell asleep around eight o'clock.

Bea dreamt about a princess who fought

dragons and won…and Juliet's sleep began with a dream of Charlie.

It was close to ten when Charlie stood staring into the darkness from his kitchen window. The tap was running and steaming water was filling the sink where he had placed his dinner dishes but it was as if he were somewhere else. Somewhere other than in his home alone, the way it was every night that he didn't work late at the hospital. The silence made him feel even more solitary but that night he chose not to have the noise of the television. He didn't want white noise providing pretend company. He suddenly felt as if he wanted something more. The lightness of heart that he felt when he was near Juliet and Bea was something he had not expected. And something he could not fully understand nor thought he deserved. He lifted his gaze to see the haze of the full moon trying to break through the heavy clouds just as he was trying to step out from behind the guilt that was burying him. But he knew he had as much chance as the moon had.

The next morning was an early start. Along with meeting with Georgina and Leo, Juliet wanted to brief the surgical team to ensure there were no questions around the procedure. Bea needed help to dress in a stretch knit track suit and then after a hearty breakfast of porridge and honey the two set off for Teddy's.

'Ith the hothpital really called Teddy'th, Mummy?'

Juliet smiled as she drove. 'Yes, it is.'

'Like a teddy bear?'

'Yes, just like a teddy bear.'

'That'th silly. It'th a hospital for babies, not for teddy bears.'

Juliet laughed along with her daughter as she turned into the hospital car park. She loved that Bea could see the funny side of life at an early age. She had taken after her grandfather with that trait and clearly the ability to make friends quickly. After the uncomfortable situation with Charlie the day before, Juliet knew she was most definitely missing that skill.

But worrying about being friends with Dr Charlie Warren was not about to take precedence over what mattered and the reason she had travelled to the *teddy bear hospital*.

The day would be busy and she had a lot to accomplish. From a risk-management viewpoint, she needed to have contingency plans in place should the babies react poorly to the procedure. While she saw no reason for it not to proceed smoothly, guaranteed success was never a given and Juliet was always prepared for both the best and worst scenarios and everything in between. Should the laser surgery initiate early labour, she wanted Charlie on the team. She just had to ask him and then wait for the lecture about unnecessary risk she knew would follow. Despite this, she would not exclude him from the theatre as she valued his skills as an OBGYN. She just hoped and prayed she didn't need to call on it.

Her mind's focus was on ensuring that it went like clockwork. There were four babies, two parents and four grandparents who were stakeholders with a heartfelt interest in the surgery being successful. Not to mention Oliver Darrington and the board who had covered the cost of her temporary relocation. The surgery would not be lengthy but it would be intricate. She intended on spending time letting the theatre staff know exactly how she operated and what she needed. She knew this would not be the first laser surgery procedure at Teddy's, but she would not take any chances with miscommunication around the operation on these babies. The staff needed to be fully aware of her expectations. She wanted Lily and Rose to grow up with their brothers, Graham and Rupert. And she would do everything in her power to make sure that happened.

It was not until she saw the black motorbike parked outside the hospital that her thoughts returned to Charlie. At least that was what she told herself, when the butterflies returned to her stomach at the sight of the shiny black road machine. She knew it wasn't the truth because she had fallen asleep thinking of him, dreamt of him and then woken with his handsome face firmly etched in her mind. She hoped he had cancelled the flowers for her office after the words they had shared the previous day. She wanted him to be spiteful and give her reason to dislike him. She didn't want to believe that underneath the gruff exterior lay a good heart. She had told herself for too many years that a man like that didn't exist and she didn't want to doubt herself.

After dropping Bea at the crèche and watching her daughter and her new best friend, Emma, hug each other excitedly, Juliet made her way to her office. She knew it was adjacent to Charlie's office. She walked past with her laptop computer under her arm ready to settle into her new workplace. As his door was ajar, against her better instincts she felt compelled to look inside. She crossed her fingers that he was not there and she did not have to address her poor behaviour first thing in the morning. This time her wish came true. Charlie was nowhere in sight. But she knew that she would have to face him. Soon. Avoiding him would only last for an hour or so as they needed to consult further on Georgina and the quads, but it would give her time to find the right words to say. An apology on her behalf was deserved. She just wasn't sure how to deliver it.

Her second wish was that the flowers were not in her office. Bracing herself, she opened the door. There was no floral arrangement in sight. Unexpectedly her heart fell. She had no idea why. It was her wish that he'd cancelled the order so she could hold that against him. But part of her had apparently, and unconsciously, hoped he wouldn't. She'd hoped he would be gallant and still have a beautiful bouquet waiting for her as a welcoming gesture. She hadn't expected it, until she'd heard about it. And at that moment she'd realised that deep inside Dr Charlie Warren was a gentleman. Despite her knowing they came from opposite sides of opinion, the fact that he had arranged an office for her and even thought of flowers made her believe in chivalry.

If only for a second.

But the lack of flowers, she knew, was fed by her own actions. She tried to remind herself it was only flowers, but the fact there were none still stung. For a few wonderful moments when she'd realised he had gone to the effort and trouble for her, she had felt special.

And she could not remember the last time a man had made her feel that way.

But it wasn't to be, Juliet decided as she dropped her oversized shoulder bag on the chair and her computer bag on the desk. Charlie had chosen to cancel the flowers, or perhaps give them to someone else. There would no doubt be a number of young women in the hospital who would be flattered to receive them. Perhaps he was even dating one of them. With his looks and position he would be quite the catch, she thought. But she wasn't fishing. She was very happy to live her life without a man who might disappoint her. She and Bea would be happy together.

And she didn't need any flowers.

She was glad she hadn't dressed in something as figure hugging as the previous day. There was no point. She was at the hospital to concentrate on the quads and nothing else. Juliet hung up her heavy overcoat on the coat stand near her desk, then smoothed down her black woollen skirt and checked her black-and-white-checked blouse was still properly tucked in. She did have very pretty black patent pumps with a kitten heel, so she hadn't entirely tried to hide her femininity. And she was also wearing her signature French fragrance. It was light and floral.

She remembered reading in one of her self-help books that she'd purchased when her trust in men had been broken four long years before that, *'When there isn't a man in your life to make you feel special, expensive perfume can.'*

She wasn't sure it would fill the void for ever, but it had worked up to that point.

Checking her emails, she noticed that Oliver had scheduled a meeting with the surgical team. She had sent a list of required staff for the procedure the day before. She'd wondered if she should consult with Charlie as the OBGYN about it, then decided it might become another debacle so decided to consult with Oliver. She was looking forward to getting to know the team and going over the procedure so that the babies had the optimum chance at leading normal, healthy lives. She couldn't see Charlie's name on the list and wondered if he had chosen to withdraw or if Oliver had made that decision for him.

Suddenly, there was a knock on her open door. She lifted her eyes to see the freshly shaven, impeccably groomed subject of her thoughts. His crisp white shirt highlighted his slightly olive complexion, and once again his blue eyes caught her attention. They appeared even more vivid from across the room.

'May I come in?'

'Of course,' she said, trying to keep the rhythm of her heart from racing and bringing a blush to her cheeks. She doubted she would be successful so she launched into the much-needed apology. 'I'm very sorry about yesterday. I behaved so poorly and I'm not sure how to make it up to you. It was professionally reprehensible, not to mention just plain awful, on my part to speak to you that way after you had made the effort to deliver the Abbiatis' decision in person.'

Charlie stood in silence for a moment and she was unsure how he would react.

'Apology accepted, Juliet,' he said, taking long purposeful steps across the room and very quickly closing the gap between them. His cologne filled those senses that his very being hadn't already claimed. 'You travelled a long way, it can't have been easy without much notice and I'm sure you have a lot on your mind. Let's just agree to disagree. I will not change my mind about the surgery and you, I can very clearly see, do not agree with the benefits of waiting.'

'You're right,' she returned. 'And it's very generous of you to accept my apology. I'm honestly not normally so rude—in fact I don't think I'm ever really rude at all. *Normally.*' Normally covered many different things for Juliet that day. Quite apart from not *normally* hopping on a plane with less than a day's notice, *normally* she didn't find herself fighting her attraction to a colleague.

'Let's call a truce,' he replied.

'Done,' she agreed, hoping that the heat she was feeling hadn't made her cheeks glow.

'I have something for you in my office. I'll be back, then we can discuss the Abbiatis.'

'Sure,' Juliet responded, not entirely sure at all what Charlie had for her but suspecting it was the update on the quads' condition. Juliet prayed it had not worsened during the night. She had intended on heading to Georgina's room as soon as she had read her emails. She wanted to speak in more depth with both Georgina and Leo about the surgery that was scheduled in two days. The risks needed to be explained again and the permission signed for surgery. Both parents had to accept that, while this was the best way forward, there would still be risks.

Juliet was deep in thought when she heard Charlie return. With a large arrangement of the most beautiful flowers.

'Oh, my goodness,' she said, getting to her feet as she watched Charlie place them on a small table by the window. 'They're gorgeous. You shouldn't have.' It was a lovely round arrangement, as if it had been picked from an English garden. Although she knew it wouldn't be from a garden in the snow-covered Cotswolds. She could see foxglove, hollyhock, snapdragon, sweet peas, roses and a few sprigs of lavender. It was the prettiest arrangement she had ever seen. And as she moved closer she could smell the delicate scent of the flowers' perfume.

'Glad you like them,' he returned. 'But I can't take the credit, since they're not from me. The board asked me to order them as a thank you for coming all this way on short notice.'

'Oh,' she mumbled, feeling silly and trying to mask the disappointment she was feeling.

'I thought I'd test the water before I brought them in case you were still upset and planned on throwing them at me. I know I didn't make it easy on you and we really did not get off to a good start.'

Juliet knew she had been crazy to think a man like Charlie Warren would buy flowers for her. She felt very foolish for thinking that he would.

'I agree we got off on the wrong foot,' she managed to reply. 'But…it's all sorted now.'

Little was truly sorted in Juliet's head. She had been entertaining romantic thoughts and even having dreams about a man who had just followed the instructions of a board and ordered flowers. At least she knew exactly where Charlie was coming from.

'Actually I haven't bought flowers since…' He paused, then stopped the conversation completely and walked to the door in silence.

Juliet thought Charlie was about to let her into something about him. The man who had an office devoid of photos or personal belongings. There was no visible history or connection to another person or persons. And no hint of a life outside the hospital. She didn't want the opportunity to know more about him to pass. 'Since?' she prompted before Charlie could leave.

Charlie drew a deep breath and turned to face her. 'Not since my wife died. There were so many flowers at the funeral that I couldn't face another flower again. Besides, there was no one to buy them for after that.'

Juliet's disappointment was quickly pushed aside by the shock of what he had said and the instinctive reaction to comfort him. She was momentarily speechless.

Her emotions were once again swinging like a pendulum.

And he was gone.

CHAPTER NINE

CHARLIE LEFT JULIET'S office before she had a chance to offer him any words of comfort or condolence. Juliet watched as he rushed out of the door, confirming matter-of-factly on the way out that they would meet with Georgina and Leo an hour later. There was no further reference to his wife or being a widower. He did not put a timeline of context to his statement. He apparently had another important appointment and one that oddly seemed to lift his spirits when he spoke about being needed elsewhere. He had quite literally dropped an emotional bombshell and run before she could say anything. The swing of the pendulum grew wider by the minute. Charlie mentioned he couldn't be late for his tough taskmaster. She couldn't think who would be harsher than himself but clearly there was someone in the hospital giving him orders. And he jumped. But jumped willingly. While the news was sad, Charlie seemed strangely upbeat as he left.

Juliet thought better than to try to learn more. He had said enough. He was a widower, and she was a single mother. Facts about each other that she had to remind herself had no relevance to their working relationship. But it was not news she had imagined hearing from him.

But it suddenly did make sense. And she could understand better why he appeared to not have a life outside Teddy's. He would have lost the life he knew when he lost his wife.

Trying to push thoughts about Charlie from her mind, she read the medical updates that had been emailed to her and sent an email to her parents, informing them that she would call in the next day or so once she had everything under control. Although she wasn't sure exactly when that would happen. She doubted while Charlie was around, or, more accurately, while she was anywhere near Charlie, that everything would be under control. He was complex and perhaps even still grieving and she was confused.

She wasn't sure she would ever really know Charlie Warren.

But she did still need to ask him to be in Theatre. She had assumed he might have attended, but after seeing the theatre staff listing and noticing his name was not there she wanted to raise it with him. It had slipped her mind in her office, but a lot did when he was around.

She had to put him back in context. He was Georgina's OBGYN and having him there would make Juliet feel more secure. She tried to tell herself it was purely from a risk-management viewpoint, but it was more than that.

With half an hour until she had to be with Georgina, Juliet decided to pop in and check on Bea. After stepping out of the elevator, she rounded the corner and saw Bea and Emma happily helping the childcare assistant to put Christmas decorations along the hallway window ledges of the crèche. It was difficult with her arm in the cast but she was managing to pass the sparkly tinsel to the young woman and Bea beamed with delight as she watched it being secured in place with tape. Juliet grew prouder of her daughter by the minute. She had adjusted to the move, albeit only for a few weeks, so well. She had made friends, not dwelled on her broken arm and was loving the opportunity to do new things.

Juliet wished she were as resilient. She was still carrying around scars that should have long healed. It was as if she had her broken heart in a cast, and she had spent almost five years dwelling on it. She certainly needed to take a leaf out of her four-year-old daughter's book on how to cope with adversity and still enjoy life. She was still allowing Bea's father to affect her life's choices. To affect the way she saw other men. She was punishing all men for the mistakes of one and feeling sorry for herself in the unnecessary process. Her daughter was a better example to her than she was being in return.

And, she quite harshly reminded herself, she hadn't lost the person she had committed to spending her life with the way Charlie had. She had been seduced and dumped by a man she barely knew and it hurt. But she had the most wonderful daughter to love while Charlie had no one. He had lost the woman he loved. His scars would with good reason run deeper. She needed to put on her 'big girl' panties and stop letting the past rule her future.

Juliet decided to get in the Christmas spirit and offer to help with the decorations. But as she drew closer she discovered the three of them had a fourth helper.

'Charlie,' Bea called out sweetly. 'We need more tinthel.'

Juliet moved back out of sight and watched

as Charlie stepped from inside the crèche and ruffled Bea's hair. 'Of course, boss. I'll get it for you now.' With that, he walked back inside the doorway and emerged carrying a large box with tinsel overflowing from the top. He placed it within Bea's little reach and then stepped back. 'Do you need any more help?'

'No, thank you, Charlie. You can go and meet my mummy about the babies but maybe you can come back and help.'

'I certainly will.'

Juliet realised the identity of the taskmaster that Charlie was meeting. She controlled the urge to laugh at the way Bea was throwing around orders and at the same time blink back tears as she watched a man who had lost his wife act almost like a father to her daughter.

Bea's banter with Charlie was so relaxed. Her orders were delivered in a cute voice, and with the best intention of getting the job done, but they were orders nonetheless. And she was only four. What made it more poignant was the fact that Charlie was taking them. She sincerely doubted anyone older than Bea could get away with being so forthright with a man like Charlie.

She suddenly worried that Bea might be auditioning him for the role of her daddy. Juliet felt torn as she walked away in silence. She and Bea would not be in the Cotswolds for ever and she didn't want her daughter to get too attached, but at the same time it was wonderful to see Bea so happy in Charlie's company. She bit her lip as she suspected with little effort it might be easy for her to become attached to Dr Warren herself. Particularly with what she now knew about him.

With her mind spinning, Juliet headed back to Georgina Abbiati's room. She needed to focus on the real reason for her travelling to Teddy's. And it was not to become involved with a complicated man. No matter how wonderfully he treated her daughter. And no matter how she felt herself warming to the handsome widower.

'So do you feel comfortable and understand fully everything I've told you about Friday's procedure?'

'I think so, Dr Turner. I mean, we've made our decision and we're not backing down now. Sorry, Charlie, but I think we've made the right decision,' Georgina said with a slight waver obvious in her voice.

Charlie nodded and, true to his word, said nothing.

'But I do have two more questions if you have time,' Georgina continued.

'Of course. I have all the time it takes to make you feel at ease and comfortable. Fire away,' Juliet said as she took one final glance at the morning's observations of her patient, including the results from the daily ultrasound she had requested. The boys' condition had remained stable and the girls were unaffected.

'I know I will have a local anaesthetic and sedation, but will I feel anything at all?'

Juliet had been asked the same question many times. 'There will be no pain, perhaps a small amount of dull tugging, but also there is a slight risk your uterus can react to any interference with contractions. Not sufficient in most cases to bring on labour but it may feel that way to you. There will be no pain, just tightness if a contraction occurs.'

'Will Charlie be in the theatre too?' Leo asked as he looked over towards Charlie. 'Just in case Georgina goes into labour.'

Juliet turned to Charlie and with equally baited breath awaited his response. She wasn't sure if Oliver Darrington was still to make the final decision on the attending OBGYN or attend himself.

'Of course,' he announced with conviction and keeping his focus on Georgina and Leo.

His words allowed Juliet to take the next breath and a smile spread over her face.

'I'm your OBGYN, and, while I have the utmost faith in the skills of Dr Turner and the team, I'm your back-up plan. If the need arises, and I'm not pre-empting it, but should the laser surgery hasten labour, I will be bringing Rupert and his siblings into the world.'

Juliet was happy with his explanation. It had not been delivered in a manner that would elevate the Abbiatis' fears, in fact just the opposite, and for that she was grateful. Charlie was playing fair.

'And I'll be very happy to have Dr Warren in Theatre. No one knows you better than your OBGYN so his presence and skills are invaluable.'

Juliet could see from the corner of her eye that Charlie had turned his head in her direction. But she didn't reciprocate. It had the potential to be a moment that she was not ready to face. Mutual admiration and respect, coupled with what she had witnessed downstairs with Charlie helping Bea. It would have been an emotional overload that she could not afford at that time.

She was feeling more than a little vulnerable. To her feelings and to Charlie Warren.

Charlie was many things and increasingly she was seeing he might even have the potential to be wonderful, but she was not looking for a man. Wonderful or not. She doubted her heart would survive. Besides, she was not staying and she did not want to start something she could not finish.

'If that's all for the moment, and you know you can page me any time, I will head off to brief the theatre staff.'

'Georgie, Leo,' Charlie began as he edged closer to Juliet's direction, 'I'm in that meeting too, so we will see you later. Rest lots, try not to stress and write down any questions so you can ask either Dr Turner or myself when we call in.'

'That went well,' Juliet began as they walked down the corridor towards the elevators. She still did not make eye contact. 'I'm glad you'll be in Theatre. It wasn't articulated on the list.'

'I was waiting to be invited. You're the lead surgeon, so it was a professional consideration on my behalf to wait until I was asked.'

'I was going to do that today.'

Charlie eyed her suspiciously. 'Well, I

guess I invited myself so, like the idea or not, I'll be scrubbing in with you on Friday.'

'I like the idea. Very much. Thank you,' she said as she pushed the button for the elevator with her pulse racing a little but a sense of contentment washing over her knowing Charlie would be there with her during the operation.

Twenty minutes later, Juliet was winding up her briefing to the theatre staff, a number of whom were pressed for time as they were due to scrub in for another procedure that afternoon. She had already gone over her theatre equipment requirements, spoken to the anaesthesia team and nursing staff. All of the medical team involved in Georgina's procedure, bar the one medical student and two interns on maternity rotation, were experienced with TTTS laser surgery, although none on more than two babies. Four was outside everyone's experience. Including Juliet's. And she did not hide that fact from the team.

'While I have performed fetoscopic laser surgery on triplets, I will not deny that on quadruplets it will be a slightly more challenging procedure. However, the direct visualisation through the fetoscope will allow us to successfully perform a targeted and fo-

cused laser termination of the vascular com-
munications directly responsible for the TTTS
and effectively separate the placenta into two
components, one for each foetus. With each
baby having its own placental mass, and the
removal of this communication, there will
be an interruption to the transfusion process
and we should stabilise the situation so we
can advance to a gestational age where the
four babies in this situation all have a greater
chance of survival. Does anyone have any
further questions?'

'If the parents of the quads did not agree
to the surgery, what would the risk be to the
other three babies if the recipient baby went
into stage five heart failure and died?'

Juliet could see the question came from one
of the interns. 'That's a very good question. If
one foetus was to become non-viable through
cardiovascular complication arising from the
TTTS, then it would put all three remaining
babies at high risk of death, injury or disabil-
ity. Essentially the fetoscopic laser procedure
has taken what was until relatively recently
a lethal placental disease and turned it into a
manageable condition if detected early.'

The specialist team were all silent. Each
nodded their understanding.

'Just one more question. If the outcome

of moving forward with this intervention is pre-term delivery, are you certain that you're sufficiently prepared for the arrival of four twenty-nine-week gestational babies with a current average weight of less than three pounds?'

Even without hearing the voice or seeing the man, Juliet knew the question had to come from Charlie, who was standing with folded arms at the back of the room. She took a deep breath. But instead of feeling resentment or interference, she appreciated the question. It was fair and one he had every right to ask in that arena and one that others might have been wondering about.

'Yes, Dr Warren, that's why we have assembled a multidisciplinary team who can deal with all potential outcomes including pre-term delivery. In addition to Ella, who is Georgina's midwife, and two anaesthetists, Mr Darrington has already approved the four neonatal intensive care nurses and two neonatologists who are here with us today, and a senior paediatrician, paediatric resident and a paediatric cardiologist, all of whom I assume you will recognise on the day but can't be at this briefing. In all we will have sixteen in the medical team, three observing and four incubators in Theatre. All of which, God willing, will be under-utilised on the day.'

Surrounded by Theatre staff, many in scrubs, Juliet suspected the imminent laser surgery for his patient became more real in Charlie's mind, giving rise to his ongoing concerns.

'Good, I'm not surprised you have it under control, Dr Turner. Let's hope we don't need any of it,' he said, then turned and walked away leaving a tiny grain of doubt in Juliet's mind.

Juliet never operated with doubt over anything. She needed to manage it immediately.

CHAPTER TEN

'CHARLIE, MAY I see you for a minute?' Juliet asked at the same time as she knocked on his open door. She had excused herself from the pre-operative meeting with the medical team and followed him back to his office. 'I need to ask your advice with regard to a question hanging over Friday's procedure.'

'What would that be at the eleventh hour?'

'It's hardly the eleventh hour.'

Charlie rolled his eyes as Juliet stepped inside his office and closed the door behind her. Normally she would have shown professional courtesy by involving him in her plans earlier but his initial reservations had ensured that did not happen. She stepped closer to his desk and looked him directly in the eyes. 'I should have asked for your input around the team. I realise it may have come across as if I've gone behind your back and made arrangements with your Assistant Head of

Obstetrics with no input from you as the quads' consulting OBGYN.'

'What's done is done,' he said as he continued rifling through the paperwork on his desk.

Juliet pulled out the chair opposite and sat down. 'I am sorry about the way I've handled this. I've been a bit like a bulldozer.'

His gaze lifted from the paperwork and met hers. 'Perhaps a mini dozer.'

She smiled. 'I really do appreciate you agreeing to be there in the surgery with me. Not for protocol…just because I need you there.' As the words slipped over her lips she surprised herself. Juliet never admitted needing anyone. And it wasn't just to make up for what she had done. She meant it. She actually needed Charlie.

He said nothing for the longest moment, leaving Juliet wondering what he was thinking.

'Let's just hope the procedure doesn't induce an early delivery because all four are too small for my liking.'

'I agree, that's why I need your advice around my contingency plan for that occurrence. Do I have everything in place? You've delivered more babies at this hospital than I've seen in my life and I'm not afraid to say that I feel a little like a fish out of water and I want your advice on how we can best prepare for the worst.'

Over the days since she had arrived, despite their disagreements, she knew Charlie was a great OBGYN. It was his passion for what he believed to be best for his patient that fuelled his stubbornness. Juliet knew he cared over and above and, while she conceded he was not one to take risks, perhaps that would make their collaboration perfect. He could temper her risks, mitigate the strategies and together they could find the best way forward.

'What is it you want to know?'

'I want to know if we have sufficient staff on board for starters. And if we don't, I need you to tell me who's missing. Oliver has left it up to me, and I would like your input.'

Finally he looked up and spoke earnestly. 'I think you're fine with the surgical team. Each and every one is the best that Teddy's has to offer and I don't think you want to further crowd the operating room. My concerns would be around the anaesthesia.'

'Why would that be?' she asked with her curiosity piqued as she shifted to the edge of her chair.

'If the laser procedure was to be the catalyst for pre-term delivery of the quads you would be looking at a Caesarean if the babies were to have any chance of surviving. They would be barely twenty-nine weeks' gestation, and babies that premature would not survive the birth canal. There would not be sufficient time for an epidural to be administered so you'd be forced to use a general.'

'So we'll have that option on hand?'

Charlie stood and walked around to the front of the desk, crossed his legs and looked directly at Juliet. 'I think you should try to avoid general anaesthesia.'

With a frown, Juliet continued the questions. 'How can we though? You just said yourself that our only option if labour was to commence as a result of the laser surgery was a GA.'

'No, I said that it would be the only option if we weren't fully prepared.'

'So you think we should have an epidural in place for the procedure rather than the local anaesthetic and conscious sedation?'

'Yes, that way we'll have both bases covered. It would meet your needs during the fetoscopic procedure, but allow a Caesarean to be performed immediately any signs of distress were detected from any of the babies.'

'It makes perfect sense.'

'Glad you agree.'

'Am I missing anything else?'

'No, I think we've covered it all now.'

They both felt the other trying to meet half-way. It was almost as if the slate had been wiped clean in a very short time by them trying to understand the other. It was starting to resemble a collaboration of minds and skills. And each of them was pleasantly surprised.

Juliet wondered fleetingly if there was a chance it could possibly become a collaboration in another sense. Then just as quickly she pushed that from her mind. She didn't need any complications in her life. And she knew Charlie Warren would be a very big complication. And if she fell for him, a very big heartache that she couldn't risk.

'I know we won't agree on the procedure,' she began with her mind back in appreciative colleague mode, 'but I value your advice. I'll meet with the anaesthetist tomorrow and brief him on the changes and then let the Abbiatis know. I'm glad we agree on this.'

'I'm glad too,' Charlie offered as he suddenly saw Juliet in a very different light. He had seen glimpses over the previous days but only in short bursts, before her need to bring home her opinion took over masking the woman he was seeing clearly again now. Suddenly he felt the defensive armour he had worn close to his chest for two years loosening a little. He had not meant to tell her about losing his wife but the words had just spilled out and he was not sorry. Letting Juliet know about his past seemed natural. In fact everything about being around Juliet suddenly seemed very natural.

'It's been a long morning,' he suddenly announced. 'And I'm quite hungry as I skipped breakfast. Would you like to join me for lunch?' He felt as if he was getting to know the real Juliet and it had been a long time since he had wanted to get to know anyone. Her interest in seeking his opinion, despite their opposing stands on the procedure, made him feel as if his advice meant something to her. And she had not pried into his personal life. He had told her about losing his wife and she had left it alone. He appreciated that respect of his unspoken boundaries.

'That would be lovely, Charlie, but I'm due to collect Bea. Would you mind if she joined us?'

'Not at all.'

Charlie was already smitten by Bea. She was a tiny version of her mother. Just as bossy, just as beautiful...and just as endearing. Her innocent joy of everything festive was making him see Christmas through her eyes instead of a man who had lost his wife at that same time of the year. The distaste he had held for anything close to celebrating was losing ground under the spell of the tiny decorator with a love of tinsel.

'Did you know that Charlie helped me with the tinthel on the windowth?'

'Did he indeed?' Juliet asked as she sipped her Earl Grey tea in the downstairs hospital tea room. Juliet did not want to let on she had witnessed Bea ordering Charlie around. It still brought a smile to her face as they sat together having a light lunch. Charlie had suggested they could head into town to have something to eat, but Juliet was well aware that he had a patient in labour and already beginning to dilate and thought better of taking him away. The roads were icy and she knew he would be taking his motorbike and the thought of him racing back in bad weather if the labour turned into a delivery without much notice did not sit well with her.

'Yeth. He was a very good helper. And he carried the boxthes.'

'Because you were a very good boss,' he said, with his eyes laughing. 'And you can't carry boxes of tinsel with a broken arm.'

Juliet laughed and looked over at Charlie.

He was the most complex man she had ever met. He had so many layers and she wasn't sure why but when he lowered his guard around Bea in particular she could see how very special he was. Juliet watched him smiling down at her daughter. His affection for her was palpable. And it made Juliet happier than she could have imagined. Not that she was looking for a father for her child, but if she had been Charlie would definitely have been a good choice.

Even Bea knew it.

'And how exactly did carting tinsel for a four-year-old became your role?' Juliet asked as she watched Bea happily sipping on her oversized chocolate milkshake. She felt certain the ladies in the tea room had found the largest cup and filled it to the brim. Bea's little legs were swinging back and forth as she gleefully watched the toy train, driven by a tiny Santa, circling a smaller Christmas tree in the corner of the tea room. Cotton wool covered the base of the tree like freshly fallen snow and it had been sprinkled with silver glitter. Juliet could see her daughter was in complete awe of it all. Juliet finally felt she could relax and exhale over her decision to bring Bea with her to the UK.

'I wanted to check on Bea's cast,' Charlie continued. 'I know you would have been keeping an eye on it, but I wanted see how my workmanship had stood up to the rigours of a four-year-old. Before I knew it I was recruited to decoration duty.'

'Be careful, knowing my daughter, she'll soon have grand plans of taking the tinsel to any part of the hospital that is not looking festive.'

'Oh, she's already scoped the entire floor and has plans of hospital-wide decorations!'

As they chatted over roast beef and mustard sandwiches all signs of animosity had abated, and for that Juliet was grateful. She could see that Charlie was a good man, a guarded, opinionated and stubborn one, with an overly cautious nature, but nevertheless a good man with a sad past. They spent a little while comparing the Australian landscape to the Cotswolds and then Charlie unexpectedly excused himself and made his way over to a very pregnant woman.

Juliet watched as he chatted with her for a moment and the two of them returned to the table.

The tall, ash-blonde woman was wearing a very tired smile and said, still chatting to Charlie, 'I can't join you but thank you for asking, Charlie. After they make my sandwich, I'll be heading home. I just finished up a long surgical repair of anomalous pulmonary veins on a newborn. It went well but I need a good sleep. I'm exhausted.'

'I'm not surprised. You're pregnant and insist on keeping up a fairly heavy surgical roster. You'll have to slow down soon,' he told her. 'But while you're waiting for your food, let me introduce you to Dr Juliet Turner and her daughter, Bea. Juliet's the *in-utero* specialist brought here from Australia to assist with the quadruplets.'

Sienna approached with her hand extended. 'Welcome aboard, Juliet. I hope you enjoy your time here.'

'Thank you,' Juliet said as she met Sienna's handshake, immediately liking the other woman.

'Sienna is Teddy's neonatal cardiothoracic surgeon,' Charlie explained. 'And one of the very best so we're fortunate to have her.'

'Said by Teddy's best OBGYN,' Charlie's very tired, very pregnant colleague told Juliet. 'But I should go… It's nice to meet you, Juliet. Perhaps we could meet up for coffee soon.'

'I'd like that, thanks, Sienna.'

'Mummy, ith that a printh?' Bea interrupted.

Juliet turned her attention to her daughter. 'Is what a prince, sweetie?'

'The man up there,' Bea said, pointing at the large television screen in the corner of the tea room. 'Ith he a printh?'

Juliet watched the news coverage and read the footnotes on the screen. 'Yes, he is a prince. It's Crown Prince Sebastian Falco of Montanari.'

'Does he have a printheth?'

'Not yet, sweetie, but he is engaged to be married and they're making quite the fuss of him. I suppose if you're a prince they will make a fuss of everything you do.'

'Will I ever be a printheth?'

'You're already *my* princess,' Juliet said as she kissed her cheek.

Sienna suddenly grabbed the seat that Charlie had offered. Juliet noticed she had also suddenly drained of colour.

'Is everything all right?' Juliet asked. 'Would you like some water? You look terribly pale.'

Charlie rushed to the cooler and, taking a bottle of water, undid the cap and passed it to Sienna. 'Get this into you.'

Juliet didn't understand what had happened as she watched the woman stare at the screen as if she had seen a ghost. She said nothing as she sipped her drink and then looked away from the screen and into the distance.

Charlie's pager abruptly beeped. 'I've been summoned. Looks like there's another baby about to enter the world. Will you be all right, Sienna? Should I get Oliver to take a look at you?'

Sienna shook her head. 'No, I'll be fine. I've suddenly lost my appetite. I really need to go home.'

Juliet walked Sienna to her car, and made sure the other woman was safely on her way. She thought that Charlie was right, that Sienna needed to look at slowing down as her pregnancy progressed. It was obviously taking its toll on her.

The next day, Juliet managed to meet with the anaesthetist to discuss the change of plans. He agreed that the dual purpose epidural would be the better option and that information would be passed on to the rest of the team. She then headed to Georgina's room to let her know the change to the preferred anaesthetic and explain the benefits of Charlie's suggestion of an epidural. The results of the daily scans were emailed through to both Juliet and Charlie and thankfully there had been no change to the TTTS status and Juliet wanted to pass this information on as well.

She checked in at the nurses' station and was told that Leo had headed home to let the family know the latest update and have a good night's sleep at Georgina's insistence. He had spent a few nights at the hospital since his return from New York and she knew he would fuss over her if he stayed that night and not get any rest himself. Juliet knocked on the door and asked if Georgina would like company.

'If you have time that would be lovely,' the mother-to-be answered as she invited her to sit for a while. 'I've been here less than a week and I'm going a little stir crazy. I can't imagine how women confined to bed for months cope.'

'You do what you have to do, and, believe me, if you were told bed rest for nine months to have healthy babies, you would do it. It's just a mother's natural instinct.'

'I suppose I would,' Georgina agreed. 'But I would still be a little loopy by the end.'

Both women laughed before turning the subject to something a little more serious. Juliet wanted to know about the supports in place for when the babies finally went home.

While it wasn't her role, she was interested to know how much assistance would be available as she reinforced the fact that four babies would be an enormous workload for the next few years.

'The babies' grandparents live very close to us, and I have a housekeeper, so I won't be struggling in terms of running the house,' Georgina answered. 'I'm very fortunate, and I know that Leo will be very hands-on too.'

'Leo's also running the family business, so he may not always be able to help, so please don't try to be brave if you feel overwhelmed at times. Let those around you know if you are struggling,' Juliet told her. 'Get extra help and take some time for yourself, even if it's just a ten-minute soak in a bubble bath. It will help you to re-energise, regroup and get right back to being a mother.'

'That sounds like you've been through it.'

'I have, believe me, but not with four babies. I only had one, she's four years old now, but it was a full-time job for me for the first few months.'

'Didn't your husband help at all?'

Juliet paused before she answered, thinking back for a moment to when Bea was a baby and then to even before that, to how scared she was as the delivery date drew closer. The fear that engulfed her some days knowing that she would be bringing up Bea alone. And how some nights she lay awake worried that she would not be enough for her daughter. That she wouldn't cope. But she did.

'I wasn't married. I'm a single mother.'

'And a surgeon,' Georgina responded. 'That's amazing. You're bringing up your daughter alone and holding down a career.'

'It's not been that difficult. Bea's almost at school now.'

'But you've done it by yourself and flew all the way over here from Australia to help my babies. I think you're the one who should take time out and have a bubble bath!'

Ella stepped into the room as the women were still happily chatting. She was there to take Georgina's blood pressure.

'I think I will head off and leave you in Ella's care,' Juliet said as she stood up to go. She wanted to go back to her office and confirm that everything was on track. 'I will see you and Leo in the morning.'

With that Juliet walked back down to her office and as usual she looked into Charlie's office as she passed by. It was a habit that had formed quickly but she was grateful he wasn't always there or it might have seemed awkward. This time he was there, sitting on the sofa with his feet up reading. It looked like a report of sorts but she didn't stop.

Not until she heard him call her name and she turned back to see him standing in the doorway.

'How are Georgina and Leo holding up?'

'Georgina's doing very well and Leo's gone home. She wanted him to rest for tomorrow,' Juliet told him, still feeling warmed by the affection the parents-to-be shared. 'They would have to be the sweetest couple, so in love and looking out for each other. Truly beautiful.'

Charlie didn't comment and Juliet suddenly felt terrible for bringing up their marital happiness. She felt so insensitive and decided to change the subject rather than add to her verbal blunder.

'What about you?' she asked to break the uncomfortable silence. 'Did the baby have an uneventful entry into the world? It must've been a quick labour for you to be back here already.'

'It was her fourth,' Charlie said, clearly keen to move away from discussing Georgina and Leo's love story. 'She was a pro. Her baby boy was delivered in forty-five minutes and she has three more at home to match. There will be no shortage of men to mow the lawns in that household.'

Juliet assumed the conversation would end there and made a mental promise to herself to be more sensitive but Charlie continued the conversation. 'Is Georgina fine with the change to the anaesthesia, then?'

She paused mid step and turned back to him, elated that there was no damage from her inappropriate comment. 'Yes, she understood why you thought it would be best. And I'm sure, because the suggestion has come from you, she feels very comfortable. I think she's happy we're working closely together—it makes her feel better about everything.'

Charlie had heard the overall details the day before but wanted some clarification around a few of the finer details. He invited her back into his office and they talked through everything from the preoperative medication to the post-operative care. He was impressed that Juliet was thorough, focused and left little to chance. It was how he liked to operate. He wasn't one to ever take unnecessary risks.

They were winding up the conversation and Juliet mentioned heading down to collect Bea. 'You apparently said you could look at staying here longer if needed to one of the midwives.'

'That's right. I'll stay until the babies are born.'

'And after that?'

'I'm not sure. If there's a position here, and the need for my skills, I may look at my options. But my family and friends all live in Perth, quite close by, which is a great support for both of us and of course my mother and father still keep watchful eyes on both of us. I'm fortunate but some may find it odd that they still fuss over me at my age.'

'Helicopter parents?'

'You could say that, but with all good intentions.'

Charlie nodded. 'Well, they let you out of their sight to make this trip at least.'

Juliet laughed. 'They actually pushed me onto the plane. I wasn't convinced that I should come here but they insisted.'

'Then they can't be too overprotective. You and Bea have travelled a long way and you're definitely not under their watchful eyes now.'

Juliet smiled. 'What about you?' she enquired. 'Are your parents here in the Cotswolds?'

Charlie's smile seemed to drop instantly. The cheery disposition Juliet had been enjoying seemed to slip away and she wished she hadn't asked. She prayed they too hadn't died. That would be a heavy burden for someone to bear. She watched as he stood up slowly and walked to the window, looking out into the distance. He didn't appear to be focusing on anything in particular.

'It's none of my business, really you don't have to answer.'

Charlie stared ahead, still saying nothing for a few moments. 'No. My parents both passed while I was in medical school. They left me a sizable inheritance to ensure I could complete my studies but they left me alone. No brothers or sisters.'

'I'm so sorry.'

'It was a long time ago and it only hits home occasionally. Usually around holidays like Christmas when it's all about family time.' Charlie rested back into his chair. 'On the subject of family, I overheard you tell the nurse in A&E that Bea only has one parent. And tell me if I'm overstepping the line but are you widowed like me…or divorced?'

Juliet reached into her bag for her bottle of water and took a large sip. She had known the subject could arise but she wished it had not been that day. She had no intention of blurting out to him details around her irresponsible one-night stand. She was a doctor and she slept with a man she didn't know and fell pregnant. Juliet accepted that it wasn't the eighteen-hundreds, as her father had often said, but the circumstance of Bea's conception, in her eyes, still made her look fairly naive and irresponsible.

Charlie was so conservative in almost every way and to announce that, *By the way I was reckless, slept with a man I barely knew, trusted him when he said he'd handled the contraception and as a result became a single mother, but the rest of the time I'm incredibly responsible...except of course for the day we met and Bea was alone in the playground and fell...and last week when I decided on a minute's notice to drag a four-year-old halfway around the world.*

Any way she looked at the situation, she felt that Charlie might judge her.

But then why did she care? His opinion shouldn't matter. But it did. She had been silly enough to trust a man who didn't deserve that trust the night Bea was conceived and naive enough to think there would be more than one night. Perhaps even forever.

She doubted that Charlie ever threw caution to the wind and for that reason she felt anxious about confessing her stupidity. But just as Charlie had told her about his wife and his parents she felt she should give him the same level of honesty.

'Bea's never met her father but he is alive

and living somewhere in Western Australia.' There it was said. Out in the open. And she knew the floodgates were also open to the barrage of questions that would follow. And she would answer all of them truthfully. Or not answer them at all.

'May I ask why?'

'It's for the best,' she mumbled. 'It's just that he's not a good person. To be frank, he's the worst type of bad.'

'Really?'

'Truly.'

'Do you want to talk about it?'

She momentarily closed her eyes and took a shallow breath. It was a risk to tell such a man about her stupid night, very stupid night with a serial womaniser. It made her appear as young and naive as she knew she looked.

'Then you don't have to…'

'No, I want to…' She swallowed pensively. 'The reason Bea's father has never met her… is because we haven't seen each other since I became pregnant.'

'So he left you when he discovered you were having his baby?'

'Not exactly. He left long before I knew.'

'How long before?' he asked.

'He left the morning after I became pregnant and he's married so there's no point going there.'

'Married?'

'He wasn't at the time…but he married a few weeks later. He was apparently engaged when we met but I had no idea. I discovered later, much later, he was a serial womaniser. He married before I had even known I was pregnant.'

'But he should have been held accountable. A man can't just walk away from the responsibility of his own child.'

That was what Juliet's father had said despite not knowing the identity of the man. No one knew the identity of the father, not even her parents. It was Juliet's secret. Perth was not a huge city and she did not want her father to confront Bea's father and tell him what he thought. It would have opened a Pandora's box and she thought that Bea might be the one to suffer the most.

'It wasn't long after the wedding I discovered he and his new bride were expecting triplets.'

'How did you discover that?'

'A cruel twist of fate had his wife's OBGYN reach out to me when a complication arose during the pregnancy. I couldn't bring myself to consult on the case so I deferred to another neonatal surgeon. How could I operate on the children of a man I despised so completely? If anything had gone wrong I feared that I'd have questioned myself for eternity and far more than anyone else ever would for sure, but it wasn't worth the risk.'

Charlie sat shaking his head. 'Still he should provide support for his daughter. It must be hard as a single mother, financially and emotionally.'

Juliet rested back into the generous padding on her high-backed chair. 'It is but I wouldn't change a thing. I adore Bea. She's my world.'

'She's adorable…despite her father. That must be because she's got more of you in her.'

Juliet smiled up at the man who was close to capturing her heart but she wasn't ready to let him. She still couldn't risk being hurt again.

'Thank you.'

'It's definitely his loss,' Charlie began before shifting the direction of the conversation slightly. 'Will you ever let Bea reach out to him?'

Juliet felt a warm feeling rush over her with his words. She would never have expected Charlie to say something like that. He wasn't judging her at all. He hadn't reacted the way she had feared.

'With three children under his belt and, from the gossip around Perth, more than a few post-honeymoon flings and another one or two since the birth of his children, I don't want him in her life. He's a real-estate developer with no conscience and both the means and opportunity to entertain other women and he's been doing that for a very long time. I will be thinking long and hard about allowing Bea to be the fourth, and unwanted, child of the man who enjoyed a pre-wedding fling with me despite having a fiancée at home waiting for him.'

'And if she asks about her father growing up?'

Juliet had not decided how she would respond when Bea asked about her daddy. And invariably she would one day.

'I'm not sure how I'll handle it. Despite my feelings about the man who fathered Bea, he's after all half of Bea and I want my daughter to grow up proud of who she is, not doubting herself because of her father's despicable behaviour. It's a dilemma I'll face later. Although I must admit recently I'm beginning to believe it will perhaps be sooner rather than later. Almost all of Bea's little friends at playgroup have fathers and Bea's beginning to talk about their *daddies*. She has a grandpa who had just retired but then… But that's another story. Anyway, he is more than thrilled to be the male role model but I know it's not the same as having a daddy.'

Charlie didn't reply. Bea was a wonderful little girl and didn't appear to be suffering from paternal neglect so obviously Juliet's father was a great surrogate. She was a sweetheart and many men would be proud to call her their daughter and watch her grow up under their watchful eye. Be there to unwrap Christmas presents together, buy her first bike and then her first car and of course scrutinise boyfriends who would never be good enough for his daughter.

Suddenly Charlie began to suspect if he wasn't careful he might just be one of those men. 'Look at the time—it's getting on and I have some paperwork to catch up on tonight at home,' he said abruptly, collected his leather briefcase, said goodnight and left his office.

Bea was happily playing in her room with cartoons on television and Juliet had just folded the last of the towels from the dryer, all the while thinking about Charlie. She could think of little else as she stacked the towels in the airing cupboard. With the empty basket in her arms, Juliet made her way into the sitting room. She could see the front porch through the lace-covered bay window.

Her jaw dropped and she almost dropped the basket when she saw who was standing on her doorstep.

CHAPTER ELEVEN

'OH, MY GOODNESS, what are you doing here?' Juliet squealed as she opened the door. She couldn't have been more surprised...or happier. 'Quickly come in from the cold!'

'It was your father's idea. He thought that we could help with Bea while you concentrate on the quads' surgery.' Her mother embraced Juliet, then stepped aside for her husband to do the same.

'It's a challenging surgery and we don't want you worrying about picking up Bea from the crèche,' her father chipped in as he carried one of the suitcases inside and then hugged his daughter warmly. He turned back for the other one still on the porch, then closed the door on the bitterly cold night air.

'Or worrying if she gets a sniffle with the sudden change in climate,' her mother added as she looked around the cosy sitting room of the cottage.

'Oh, my God, why didn't you tell me you were coming?'

'Because you would have said we were fussing—'

'Which you are…but I'm very glad you like to fuss.'

'And we missed you both terribly.'

'It's been less than a week.'

'See what an only child has to suffer. Two parents who miss you after less than a week and follow you to the other side of the world,' her father continued as he placed the second suitcase down. 'So learn from us and give Bea some brothers or sisters in the future or she'll be doomed to having a helicopter parent hovering around like us!'

Juliet smiled. 'If I'm half as good a parent as you two, then Bea will be a lucky girl.'

'We are the lucky ones, Juliet. You make us both very proud.' Her father hugged Juliet again and then stepped away a little as his eyes filled with tears of happiness.

Juliet could see the emotion choking him and knew all three of them would be a mess if she didn't change the subject. 'So when did you decide to fly out? And how did you arrange it so quickly?'

'We had passports so we just rang the travel agent. We've booked into a hotel nearby for tomorrow but they didn't have a spare room tonight.'

'You'll do no such thing. There's plenty of room here.'

'We don't want to put you out. We'll just stay tonight if that's okay. We can sleep on the sofa.'

'Don't be ridiculous. You'll stay here…now how long are you able to stay?'

'Till you get sick of us,' her mother replied.

'Then you'll be here for a long time,' Juliet said. 'What about a nice cup of tea?'

'That would be lovely,' her father said.

'Well, actually, we've booked one of those river cruises through France and Spain,' her mother added. 'That's the week after Christmas.'

'I thought you had planned that for next July? You were going to enjoy summer in Europe. Leave the Australian winter behind and thaw out over here.'

'That was our plan but we brought it forward. No point flying out twice. It's a long way for two old people.'

Juliet laughed. 'Hardly old but you'll be missing the sunshine on your cruise.'

The three of them looked up as Bea came running down the hallway. 'Grandma! Grandpa!'

'Here comes all the sunshine we need,' her father said.

Juliet's parents both dropped to the ground, her father a little more slowly due to the arthritis that plagued his knees. A group hug ensued with lots of kisses.

'I knew Father Chrithmath was real,' the little girl said with a toothy grin.

'Of course Father Christmas is real, but why do you say that?' Juliet asked as she looked at the three of them nestled together on the rug on the floor.

''Coth I asked him to bring Grandma and Grandpa here to play in the snow with me and have Christmath food and everything.'

'How did the surgery go for Kelly Lester?' Juliet asked as they sat by the fire after settling into Bea's room. Bea was happy to move in to Juliet's room and sleep in the big bed and give her room to her grandparents. 'I got your email that the procedure was successful but how is Kelly progressing post-operatively?'

'Good, very good,' her father answered as he reached for a homemade cookie. 'She's a strong woman, lots of family support and, although there will still be hurdles as to be expected with spina bifida, the chances have been greatly improved of the child walking by about the thirty-month mark, which I know was your prognosis. And we both know without surgical intervention the little boy would never have walked or really enjoyed a quality of life.'

'Look at you two. Like peas in a pod,' her mother said as she finished her second cup of tea.

'You liked the tea, Grandma?'

'Yes, I did, Bea.'

'Would you like some more?'

'No, thank you, sweetie. But what I would like is to hear about how you got that cast. Mummy rang and told us how it happened but it did sound very scary.'

Momentarily distracted from her cup of hot chocolate, Bea looked at the cast intently. 'I fell from the slide and broke my arm.'

'Are you feeling better now?' her grandfather asked as he lovingly watched his granddaughter.

'Yeth, Charlie made my pink cast.'

'It's very pretty and has lots of beautiful drawings,' her grandmother replied.

'Yeth, my friendth drew them,' Bea told them, then, pointing at the image of a sunflower, she continued. 'Thith one is by Emma, my betht friend.'

'Well, she's very clever and I'm sure very nice.'

'Charlie ith very nice too, and very tall. Like a building,' Bea said as she jumped to her feet and stretched her hand up as high as possible. 'He'th Mummy'th friend and he'th going to get us a Chrithmath tree. A really, really big one.'

'Did Charlie offer to get a Christmas tree for the house?' Juliet asked with a curious frown. He had not mentioned it to her.

'Yeth, Mummy, he told me he would get a beautiful tree for uth.'

Juliet's parents looked at each other with a knowing smile.

'Don't go there,' Juliet said, shaking her head. Since the strange way he'd left off with Juliet, she wasn't sure about him. She felt that he was hiding something from her and she wasn't sure she wanted anyone that complex in her life. 'He's the OBGYN, and to be honest, most of the time, quite difficult to work with. It's taken almost all week to finally come close to understanding him. He's conservative and stubborn and fought me every inch of the way about the *in-utero* surgery.'

'Why did he attend to Bea? Since when do OBGYNs attend to paediatric fractures?'

Juliet drew a deep breath and put down her

spoon. 'He's the doctor that rushed to Bea in the playground. The doctor I was waiting for inside and he was running late. He arrived at the hospital at the same time Bea fell.'

'Serendipity…'

'Mum, please, I said don't go there.'

'Is he handsome?'

'Mum…'

'It's a simple question, Juliet. Is the nice doctor who saved Bea, and is now, according to our granddaughter, *your friend*, who is going to buy you a Christmas tree, handsome?'

Juliet swallowed. 'Yes, he's handsome… and incredibly difficult at times—'

'And also with a very kind streak by the sound of it too,' her mother cut in.

Juliet's eyebrow was raised as she returned her attention to the last few crumbs of cookie on her own plate. She wasn't going to get into an argument. Her mother had said the truth. Charlie did have a chivalrous and kind side to him and she didn't want to think about that.

'He'th nice,' Bea added, completely oblivious to her mother's opinion of Charlie. 'We put up tinthel, and pretty thingth around the hothpital.'

'Really? Not what I would have thought was part of an OBGYN's job description?'

her mother said without making eye contact with Juliet.

'Particularly not one who's difficult...' her father mused, looking at his wife.

'Let's not forget stubborn,' her mother commented with a wistful smile.

Juliet stood up. 'Have you finished?'

'With this conversation or the cookies?' her mother asked with a cheeky grin.

'Both!'

'Remember, if there are any issues or just for peace of mind, if you need or want to stay at the hospital and monitor the quads' mother, you know your mother and I are here to look after Bea.'

'I still can't believe you flew all that way just so I could focus on the babies,' Juliet said as she gathered the last of her things, wrapped her scarf around her neck over her heavy coat, pulled on her knitted cap, kissed Bea and headed for the door. They had all enjoyed a restful night's sleep and Juliet felt good about the impending surgery.

'If Bea needed you in the future, you would do exactly the same.'

Juliet knew that was the truth. She would indeed do anything for her daughter, at that time or any time in the future.

'Despite what you say, Juliet,' her mother added as she sipped her early morning cup of tea and prepared for the cold gust of air as her daughter opened the door, 'it's not easy being single and raising a daughter and having a career that makes you responsible for other people's lives. You have a lot on your very slender shoulders.'

'But I love it. It gives me purpose and I can't imagine doing anything else,' Juliet told them both as she stepped onto the porch and closed the door behind her.

'I know,' her mother replied as she looked over at her husband, reading the local paper. 'The apple indeed did not fall too far from the tree.'

Georgina and Leo were waiting outside Theatre when Juliet arrived. With her hair tucked inside a disposable cap, and dressed in a hospital gown, Georgina had been prepped for the surgery. She was lying on the trolley with the sides up ready to be wheeled inside by the theatre staff. Leo was holding his wife's hand tightly and trying to put on a brave face but Juliet could sense the fear that was mounting by the minute.

'I will be scrubbing in for your procedure now,' she told them as she patted Georgina's arm. 'And, Leo, you can scrub in with me. I know that Georgie will want you right beside her during the procedure.'

'Sure.'

'Any questions?'

'Yes,' Leo said with a cheeky smirk. 'How hot does it get in Australia in summer?'

Juliet was surprised by the question. It was definitely left of centre. 'Quite hot in Perth, well over one hundred degrees on our hottest days. I left only a few days ago and we'd been through a heatwave—we had three days in a row that reached over one hundred and five degrees.'

'That's hot. Maybe spring would be nicer.'

Aware that time was ticking, and the medical team would be waiting, she quickly asked, 'For what, exactly?'

'Georgie and I have decided, should all of our babies come through this happy and healthy...' he paused for a moment and smiled lovingly at his wife '...that in honour of you we're going to take them all on a trip to Australia before they start school. We were planning on showing them Italy, but I think an adventure down under would be more fun for the six of us. Besides, Georgie and I have been back to Italy a few times but we've never seen a kangaroo up close and we can tell the girls how an Aussie doctor saved their brothers and, if you're home, perhaps we could call in and say hello.'

Juliet thought it was such a sweet sentiment and optimistic. It was what would pull them through whatever lay ahead. 'And I will put the barbie on for all of you.'

'I'll cook the pasta,' Georgina added from the trolley.

'And I'll bring the vino,' Leo chipped in as the theatre staff began to wheel his wife into surgery. Juliet couldn't help but see through his jovial façade that a tear trickled down his cheek. She patted his arm. 'Georgina is in good hands and so are your babies.'

Juliet then took Leo to scrub in.

'Heads up to the medical student and interns with us today, if you have questions about any of this procedure, ask. We will be using a laser to coagulate the shared blood supply between two of the four babies. This will be more complex with the four foetuses and will take considerable time to map the shared arteries and veins but it will be done. So we are all in here for the long haul.'

Charlie was pleased to hear the conviction in Juliet's voice.

'After this procedure I am hoping the two

babies currently affected by the TTTS will be able to grow to their maximum size without complications.'

The epidural had taken effect and Leo was behind the blue surgical sheet holding his wife's hand. Everyone present in Theatre was wearing the protective goggles in preparation for the laser, including Georgina and Leo. Juliet carefully inserted the fetoscope and, guided by the screen, began the arduous task of locating Rupert, otherwise known as Baby A. Once this was done she traced his umbilical cord back to the placenta and began the process of identifying the offending arteries. Secure in the knowledge she had the first communication located, Juliet utilised the laser to cauterise the artery.

Charlie held his breath. That was only the first; he was well aware there were more to locate and sever. Juliet continued mapping the vascular placental linkages and painstakingly cauterising each one. The procedure was progressing slowly but successfully. Charlie was still cautious. Any disruption to the uterus he knew was risky. With only two veins to cauterise, Juliet announced they were on the home stretch and everyone in Theatre felt instant relief sweep over them.

'Well done, Juliet,' the anaesthetist announced. 'Great outcome.'

'I said home stretch, not completed,' she countered cautiously as she pushed down on the foot pedal for the laser and severed the second to last. 'We still have one to go.'

Charlie was impressed with her reply. She had every reason to gloat that close to seeing the end in sight but still she was hesitant to accept praise. He also realised that he had been wrong to judge the procedure. Perhaps, in fact, Juliet had made the right call with the quads. And if the babies all continued to grow, they would be able to prolong the pregnancy for at least a few more weeks until the uterus became too large, but by that time the babies would be all viable and have a good chance at a healthy life.

The final artery was the most difficult to locate due to Baby B's position. All eyes were on the monitor as Juliet carefully manoeuvred around the tiniest twin.

'We have a problem,' the neonatal cardiologist announced. 'Baby B's struggling, he's clearly in stress.'

Charlie stepped forward again to observe the screen. The invasive procedure had been delayed by the fact it was four babies, not two, and it had adversely affected the smallest quad.

'I'm ceasing laser now,' Juliet told the room, then quickly but delicately removed the fetoscope but it was too late. Without warning Georgina's water broke. The operating table was saturated with the amniotic fluid of the boys. The girls, in a separate sac, were unaffected but that would not mean they were safe. If the boys were to be born, so would the girls.

'I'll take over from here. We're in labour and delivering,' Charlie announced as he removed his protective laser glasses, switched them for clear glasses and stepped up to the operation table. He looked over the blue curtain to the Abbiatis. 'Georgie, Leo, your children are on their way,' he said, before turning his attention back to the immediate task. 'Nurses, please prepare for a Caesarean section—we have four twenty-nine-week foetuses that are neither large nor strong enough to pass through the birth canal.'

Immediately Juliet stepped back as she watched the surgical tray swing around in reach of Charlie. She approached Georgina and Leo, leaving the operation table free for Ella and the other midwife to approach and assist.

'The epidural was our safety net,' Juliet said softly. 'It won't be too long before your babies are born.'

'But…they're…too…tiny,' Georgina stated with fear paramount in each staggered word.

'They're small but, thanks to Dr Warren's suggestion of the epidural, we're more than adequately prepared. There'll be no delay in delivering all four babies and that is an important factor. They will be assessed by the neonatal team and then moved quicker to neonatal ICU.'

Carefully but with haste appropriate to the situation, Charlie made the first incision at the base of Georgina's engorged stomach, cutting through the outer layer of muscle. Then carefully he prised open the first incision to reveal the almost translucent uterus that had been stretched to capacity with the four babies. Once through to that layer, Charlie cut the unbroken amniotic sac of the girls, and, reaching in, he carefully pulled free the first of the tiny infants. Carefully he placed the baby in the first neonatal nurse's hands while he clamped the umbilical cord. One clamp for the first baby, who was named by the team, Baby C. The second girl followed a few minutes later; it was Baby D and she had two clamps. Baby D was slightly larger and began to cry immediately. Quickly she was taken by the second midwife. Then came Baby A and finally the smallest of them all, Baby B, who had been against his mother's spine. Removing him from the womb proved tricky as he was the smallest and the most fragile. She could see the concern in Charlie's eyes but along with it was sheer determination. Finally he was pulled free, blue and almost translucent, but alive.

Juliet watched in awe as Charlie tenderly held the tiny infant while the final cord was clamped. The paediatric team worked alongside the neonatal nurses to assess all of the babies. But it was Baby A that caused the greatest concern. He had been the recipient baby and, while not the smallest, his heart had been pumping furiously for the previous twelve hours as Georgina had teetered on the periphery of stage five.

Charlie's focus remained with Georgina. There were still two placentas that needed to be delivered and then the painstaking work of closing the Caesarean section. Juliet remained with Georgina and Leo. It was where she was most needed at that time. With a heartfelt admiration for Charlie, she watched as he expertly began to repair the opening that had allowed Lily, Rose, Rupert and Graham to enter the world.

'You're an incredibly skilled obstetrician and you have no idea how very grateful I am that you were in Theatre today,' Juliet commented as she removed the disposable gown over her scrubs. 'I'm just sorry you had to use your skills.' She was waiting for what she knew would follow. And what she knew would be a fair call. *I told you so.*

But it didn't. Instead, she received the most unexpected praise.

'I did okay, but your skills are second to none, Juliet. I observed you mapping the placenta's vascular pathways. Not an easy task with two babies, but with four it was a miracle and you managed to cauterise all but one artery. And if you'd been provided the time then the quads would still be happily tucked inside Georgina for another few weeks. But fate had another idea.'

Juliet pulled her surgical cap free. 'So you're not upset that I tried. I thought you would be…and justifiably so.'

Charlie turned to face her. 'The opposite, actually.'

'Now I'm confused.'

'If you hadn't pushed for the fetoscopic laser surgery, Juliet, then Rupert's heart would've remained overworked for another twelve hours and it might have been too late. We wouldn't have done another scan until tomorrow and there's every chance he would have gone into heart failure during the night. We would not have had the opportunity to save him.

'I'm very glad you came all the way from Australia to fight me on this. You saved at least one baby's life. If not all four.'

CHAPTER TWELVE

'THANK YOU, CHARLIE. That was an unexpected compliment.'

'Perhaps unexpected but not undeserved. I think you know me well enough after the last few days together to know that I don't hold back my opinion, whether others want to hear it or not. In this case I hope you want to hear it. And while I didn't initially agree, you proved me wrong and that rarely happens.'

'As I said, your compliment was unexpected but very much appreciated,' Juliet said as she removed her surgical gloves and dropped them in the designated bin along with her surgical cap and gown. 'There were a few scary moments in there and I must admit I felt a little out of my depth more than once.'

Charlie slipped his surgical cap free and ran his fingers through his hair. 'You seemed pretty poised and in control even when it all went south.'

'I may have looked composed but my mind was the duck's feet paddling underneath at a million miles an hour. You were the star today.'

Charlie smiled at her analogy and Juliet thought it was the most incredible smile.

'Seriously, you need to take credit where it's due. Teddy's are so fortunate to have you on staff. You could move permanently to anywhere in the world. There would be so many hospitals that would love to steal you, of that I'm sure.'

'What about you?' he answered quickly, still looking into her eyes with an intensity she had not experienced.

The deep blue pools were threatening to pierce the last barriers of resistance to him. Watching him so expertly and confidently lead the team and deliver the four babies safely had brought a new level of admiration for him that she knew few, if any, other doctors could surpass. But Juliet still wasn't sure what he meant. Was he asking if she wanted to steal him? The answer of course would be yes, if she could dull the alarm bells ringing in her head and bury her doubts.

'I'm not sure what you mean?' she asked nervously.

He crossed his arms across his impressive

chest and stepped out his legs. It was a powerful stance not lost on Juliet.

'I mean, would you seriously consider living and working here? Would you let Teddy's perhaps steal you permanently from your base in Perth?'

'I'm not sure.'

Juliet felt the intensity of his gaze upon her. She wasn't sure if he was waiting for her to say anything as he stood looking at her without saying a word. She felt her pulse quicken and she became almost breathless with him standing so close to her. Her skin tingled and he had not touched her. She wondered for a moment if she would or could say no to him touching her if they were somewhere else alone…and he tried to pull her to him.

'Are you hungry?'

Juliet was taken aback by his question. *Hungry for what?* Her eyes widened and she felt excitement surge through her veins as she nodded.

'What if I cook us dinner at my place?'

'Your place?'

'Yes, my home's twenty minutes from here. You could follow my bike and I could whip us up something half edible and definitely better than the vending machine, which is your other choice if you stay here at this time of the night.'

'But what about Bea…?' she began to ask as her chest rose with a nervous intake of air.

'I don't think your parents will let her starve and they've more than likely eaten already. Bea may even be in bed asleep. It's almost eight o'clock.'

Juliet hadn't realised the time. It was true, it was late, and they all might have been asleep, not just Bea. She was trying to keep her emotions in check and remember it would be merely a dinner shared by two colleagues. She just had to keep remembering that fact and everything would be fine.

'Give me fifteen minutes to have a quick shower and change.'

'Of course. I could do with a hot shower to loosen my muscles as well. I'll meet you in your office in twenty minutes.'

Juliet walked away knowing she hadn't wanted anyone's company in a very long time. Not until that moment.

Juliet followed behind Charlie's bike along the winding road. The moon's halo lit his broad masculine silhouette as they travelled slowly through the darkened countryside. There was no other traffic, just the two of them on the road. Juliet felt herself mesmerised as he leaned into the turns and curves of the road. His was agile and strong and completely in control of the huge machine. He made it impossible for her not to stare in awe and a little bit of anticipation as he led her to his home.

Finally they pulled into the large estate and Juliet wondered if he had one of the cottages, but soon learned it was the stately mansion that was indeed his home. Even with just the moon lighting the grounds, she could see how magnificent the landscape and how grand his home.

'This is beautiful,' she said as she climbed from the car wearing jeans, a pullover and boots. Her hair was tied up in a makeshift ponytail and a thick scarf and coat rested on her shoulders. 'I've never seen anything quite like it.'

'It's a work in progress.'

'It looks wonderfully finished to me,' she replied as she followed him up the steps to the two-hundred-year-old home. 'It's simply glorious. Nothing quite like it in Perth.'

Charlie unlocked the door and held it open for Juliet to enter, before he stepped inside and closed the door. 'I'll put on a fire and start dinner then show you around, if you'd like.'

With her gaze scanning the furnishings and architecture of the beautiful interior, she nodded. 'I'd love that.'

The fire was roaring and the meat was ready whenever they were; it would take only a few minutes on the grill. Charlie reappeared in the doorway, aware that he was not in a hurry to cook or rush anything about the evening. The surgery, and everything that had happened over the last few days since meeting Juliet, had made him feel alive and made him hunger for more time alone with her, despite his better judgement. 'Would you like a glass of wine?'

'I do have to drive home.'

'Not for a while. Besides, you'll be eating and I'll give you only half a glass.'

'That sounds lovely. I won't head in until around one tomorrow so it might be nice to let my hair down.'

Charlie smiled. Seeing *Juliet* on the sofa, with her beautiful face lit by the fire, was a sight he had never imagined over the years of his self-imposed solitude. But it was a sight he was relishing. 'I'll be back.'

Juliet looked into the crackling fire and as another log was consumed by flames she thought how very different Charlie was from the man she'd first met. In five short days he had opened up and shown a compassionate, loving side completely at odds with the brusque exterior he had first displayed. Bea was smitten by him, and she felt sure if her parents met him they too would think he was very charming. An English gentleman with an English country manor. It was all very proper and lovely. A little like a fairy tale but she wasn't yet sure of the ending. Or indeed if fairy tales happened.

Charlie appeared with two glasses of red wine, Juliet's only a quarter filled.

'As I promised,' he said as he handed her the long-stemmed Waterford Crystal glass. Their hands touched as he gave her possession of the cold crystal and it instantly stirred an overwhelming desire to feel more than just her hand against his. His mouth immediately craved Juliet's full, inviting lips hovering only inches from his own. He let his gaze linger for a moment on her mouth, all the while wondering if it would taste as sweet as it looked. He pushed the cold rim of the glass against his mouth in a bid to control the mounting desire surging through his veins.

'Thank you,' she said as she climbed to her feet. 'Can I have the grand tour now? Do we have time?'

'All the time in the world,' he replied.

* * *

Charlie led Juliet around the ground floor. Leaving the generous sitting room, he showed her the kitchen with the butler's pantry, the dining room, which she noticed had been set for two, the utility room, a wonderfully inspiring floor-to-ceiling library, a study with a large oak desk and bookcase and a billiard room that housed an antique snooker table. As they entered each room he thought about kissing Juliet but then reasoning stepped in and made him keep a little distance. But each room was harder than the last.

'You said you were renovating but it all looks perfect to me.'

'I finished downstairs first then moved upstairs with the repairs and redecorating.'

'What's upstairs?' she asked, her curiosity driving her towards the staircase. She was fascinated by the house and couldn't wait to see more.

'The seven bedrooms,' he answered as he followed her lead and moved towards the grand staircase. 'Apparently all of them including the master bedroom are finished but I haven't seen them yet.'

Juliet thought the statement was odd and turned to him. She said nothing as she assumed he had been too busy to check it out, but she couldn't imagine not rushing home to see the progress every night, no matter what the time of day. He was very low-key.

'So where do you sleep?'

'Over there,' he said, pointing at the chesterfield. 'I'm accustomed to it now. I've been sleeping there for a few months while the work's been happening upstairs.' Charlie didn't tell her that he didn't feel any motivation to sleep in the new master bedroom alone.

'It's a very comfortable sofa, but if the master bedroom's finished then it's time you moved in. Let's take a peek.'

Charlie noticed everything about Juliet as she climbed the stairs ahead of him. Her slim hips swaying in her tight jeans with each enthusiastic step, the way her curls bounced when her head flicked from side to side as she looked at the antique framed paintings hanging on the wall, and the slender fingers of one hand gliding up the balustrade, the other hand encircling her glass. She was gorgeous, intelligent and sexy. And watching her, he suspected he was smitten. He wasn't sure if it could be more than that but it was still more than he had imagined ever feeling again.

By the time they had reached the large oak door of the master bedroom, Charlie knew he couldn't resist her any longer. He wanted to spend the night in the refurbished room. But not alone. He wanted to spend the night with Juliet. She had made him feel more alive than he had in years. She, and her little girl, had made him believe there could be life outside the hospital. He had been alone for so long, but now this sexy, desirable woman had stirred feelings that he'd never thought he would feel in his body and soul the way he did at that moment. And if all they had was that moment, he couldn't let it slip away without taking a chance.

Juliet tentatively opened the heavy door to the darkened room and Charlie brushed her shoulder gently as he reached around for the light. Her heart unexpectedly began to race with his touch. Nervously she swallowed and bit the inside of her cheek. She was at the entrance to Charlie's bedroom and she couldn't see anything. But she realised that she wasn't scared.

She couldn't see the future but suddenly that didn't matter either. She didn't need to have everything laid out. She felt safe. Safer than she could remember feeling before. The fleeting warmth of his body against hers caused butterflies to stir. As each second passed with him so close to her, she loosened her tether to fear. Pushing away the promises she had made to never trust again. With his warm breath on her neck, she felt herself feeling free to fall into whatever this could be. She didn't want to run away from her feelings.

As his fingers flicked on the light switch, Juliet found herself looking around at the elegant decor, in the soft lighting. But her focus was the imposing four-poster bed that dominated the room...and dominated her thoughts. It could be their bed for the night.

Suddenly everything felt right. The man standing so close to her was everything she could hope for and he was within her reach.

That bed would be theirs.

Her breathing became laboured with anticipation as she felt Charlie's strong hands on her hips. Gently but purposefully he swivelled her around to face him. Her mouth was only inches from his and it made the ache inside her almost overwhelming. With only the sound of their hearts beating, he searched her face for permission to kiss her and she smiled her consent as she reached up on her tiptoes to meet his lips. Taking her glass and placing it with his on the large oak dresser, Charlie scooped her up in his arms and carried her to the bed, where he laid her down and gently began to peel away her clothing. He slipped off her boots, tugged down her jeans and then slid her arms and body free of her jumper, revealing her white lace underwear.

Juliet watched and admired as he pulled free all of his own clothing, discarding each piece roughly to the floor. Finally, gloriously naked, he loosened her hair from its ponytail and then began to slowly remove the last remnants of clothing keeping them apart. With every part of his mouth and body he began to pleasure Juliet in ways she had not thought possible and ways she did not want to end. Willingly and wantonly, she gave into all of her desires for the man who had awakened the woman in her. And over the hours he loved her that night she gave a little part of her heart to him as they crossed the divide from colleagues to lovers.

Charlie looked over at Juliet still asleep. She was beautiful and loving and everything a man could desire. She had given herself to him willingly and, while it had been the most amazing night, in the soft light streaming from the hallway his actions hit home hard. He had taken the chance. For the first time in a very long time he hadn't denied his feelings but as he lay there looking out into the still of the darkness outside he knew he should have fought this harder. He should never have invited her to dinner, let alone to his bedroom. He regretted everything about the night. The sight of her peacefully sleeping tugged at his heart. A heart so damaged that it hadn't felt anything but pain for so long.

And now the pain returned two-fold. He had betrayed his resolve to live his life without love out of respect for Alice and now there was a second burden. He would be forced to hurt Juliet. A very special woman he did not want to hurt. A woman who did not deserve to be hurt. She was loving and trusting and she had given herself to him openly and honestly. He knew everything there was to know about her.

But she did not know everything about him. She had no idea that he could not let her into his life. Last night was all they would share. He could not accept happiness. He didn't deserve it. As he felt the warmth of her body against his he suddenly felt overwhelmed by the guilt that had been his constant companion for two years. Thoughts of Juliet and what might have been had their lives been different filled his mind. Her scent was on every part of his body and buried the guilt for those few hours but he knew it was only temporary. It wouldn't last and then he would bring her down too. She deserved better than to be with a man who would never be free to love her. He had to set her free.

'Good morning,' she softly said as she lifted herself up to meet his lips.

His mouth felt the warmth of hers but he ended the kiss before it deepened. The need for her was as strong in the morning as the night before but now he knew he had to fight it. It should never have gone that far.

'I'm sorry I fell asleep. I should have left a while ago. You invited me for dinner, not a sleepover.'

He sat bolt upright. If he held her close to him he would give in to his desire. He would take her again and feel her warm soft skin against his and that would make what he had to do more difficult. And more painful for both of them.

'That was my fault as much as yours. I guess we just got carried away by the heat of the moment. Yesterday was quite an intense day. But I'll get you some breakfast before you leave,' he told her as he lifted the covers, swung his legs down and found his boxer shorts and then a heavy winter robe lying on the chair beside the bed. 'I'm sure I can rustle up some toast for us. I'm going to head into the hospital and check on the quads and my other patients.'

'Is there something wrong?'

'No,' he lied. 'I just think we should get going. Last night was…well…special but I'm sure you agree not something we should repeat. It'd make working together difficult for the short time you still have here and neither of us would want that.'

Each word was carefully chosen to hide any level of emotion. What he wanted to do was to pull her into his arms and make love to her again, but he couldn't. He couldn't surrender to the emotions surging through him after they'd spent the night together. He feared his heart and soul were still in pieces and he needed to accept that in the harsh light of the morning. He was damaged and she needed a man who was still whole. Her tenderness and honesty made him feel worse. But he couldn't prolong what he knew he had to do. End it before it began. Not because he didn't care about her but because he feared caring too much.

'I'm really confused, Charlie. I won't lie,' she said as she pulled the covers up around her. 'After last night and…after what happened between us, why are you so distant to me this morning? You sound so cold and…

just nothing like you were last night. Why are you in such a hurry for me to leave?'

'I'm not being cold. I'm being honest. Last night was great but we both need to see it for what it really is.'

'And what is that?'

'A great night together—'

'A one-night stand?' she cut in.

'Juliet, it was fantastic,' he said. 'But we're colleagues and I'm not looking for a relationship. I think the intensity of what we went through yesterday with the delivery of the quads heightened our emotions and we acted upon it.'

'So last night was just a fling after the surgery, a reaction to a successful outcome? Is that how you see it?'

Charlie used every ounce of his strength not to reach for her. Not to say how he really felt. Not to let her know that she was breaking through his defences and making him want more. That there was no one he wanted to be with more than her. But he couldn't.

'You can and will do far better than me. I was just for last night.'

'So in your mind it really was just a one-night stand?'

'That doesn't sum up what we shared...'

'But it's how you see it,' she spat back angrily.

'Well…'

'I can't believe this,' she said with anger and disappointment colouring her tone. 'You're no different from all the other men who want a quick roll in the sack with no strings attached—'

'That's not true.'

'Tell me how it isn't true. If this was only for one night then you should have let me in on that fact yesterday, before we fell into bed together. I thought we shared something more than that, or at least we could, given time.'

Charlie hated what he had to do and say. His heart wrenched. This woman was wonderful and loving but he could never be what Juliet needed.

'I didn't mislead you, Juliet. I don't think either of us thought too much about anything other than being with each other but now, in the light of day, we have to be practical. I need to be alone and you're not staying in the UK long term so let's not delay the inevitable.'

What he wanted, with all of his still unhealed heart, was to say that spending any more time with her and knowing he had to let her go would be unbearable. He was torn between the happiness that he felt around her and the guilt that he knew he deserved to carry.

The guilt that would ruin any chance for them having any sort of a future.

'Charlie, does this have something to do with your wife? Lots of people lose their partners but they go on to love again.'

'That has nothing to do with this,' he lied again. 'It doesn't matter why, it's just the way it is.' His voice was shaky as he tried to hold back what Juliet did not need to know.

'I'm not buying it. I think I know you almost better than you know yourself, even though that sounds ridiculous after a week but it's how I feel. So I need to know something. I need you to tell me what happened, Charlie,' she said. Her tone had softened. 'What happened to your wife? Because that has everything to do with your need to be alone. I know it has.'

Charlie's back stiffened and his jaw tensed. 'It won't change anything.'

'Perhaps not, but I want to know.'

He climbed from the bed and began to gather his clothes in silence. He did not want to open up old wounds.

'Charlie,' Juliet began as she leant against the bed head, the bedclothes wrapped around her still-naked body. 'I'll go. I know you want me to leave but you owe me an explanation for what is happening now. I need to know why you're rejecting us…and why you won't even try.'

'Fine,' he said as he inhaled and filled his tight chest with air and stood in the middle of the softly lit room staring back at Juliet. 'You know I'm a widower and you know my wife, Alice, died two years ago. It was a car accident that claimed her life on the road that leads out of town. She died in the Cotswolds only two miles from this house and I wish every day that I could change places with her but I can't. She died and I am forced to live on.'

Juliet sat for a moment in silence. 'Charlie, I'm sorry that you lost your wife so tragically, but you can't change what's happened or trade places with her. Do you think she would want you to be living with that much sadness? Don't you think you're being hard on yourself? You're still here and you can live your life…'

'After I took hers? I don't think so.'

'What do you mean, after you took hers? It was an accident.'

'I was driving.'

'Were you drunk?'

'No,' he spat angrily. 'I would never get behind the wheel if I'd been drinking.'

'Then it wasn't your fault.'

He stood rigidly. 'She was excited about going to the dinner. I couldn't have been further from excited. The weather had been the worst we'd seen in years, I'd been in surgery all day and wanted to stay home but I didn't want to refuse her. I didn't want to appear selfish so I gave in. When I should have said no, I said yes. Despite my reservations, we headed out on the snow-covered roads, I lost control and I killed her.'

'No, Charlie, you didn't kill her. The weather, the road, fate, that is what killed Alice. You can't take responsibility for that. Factors came together to take her life.'

He paced the room. His hands were clenched tightly. 'We shouldn't have been on the road, in the weather. I should have been more cautious. I should've protected her. I was her husband; that was my role.'

'I bet you had driven in that weather many times without incident and you thought that night would be no different...'

'But it was different. I should've argued the point, and insisted we stayed in, out of the weather.'

'Even if you had done that, you know Alice

could have been in an accident the next morning travelling to work. It could have happened any time. Or worse, she could have gone on her own and you wouldn't have been there for her. You tried to protect her. You were tired and yet you agreed and did your best to protect her by being with her.'

'But I failed and nothing you say can change this. I've felt this way since the day she died and I will feel this way until the day I die. And it's the reason I haven't driven in more than two years. I won't get behind the wheel of a car again. Ever. Please, Juliet, I think it's best that you leave.'

'Charlie, we can talk about this—'

'No.' He knew his coldness wasn't lost on Juliet and he wanted it that way. He had to push her away before he fell too hard and couldn't let her go. 'There's nothing else to say. I'm sorry if you were looking for more. But I'm not and never will be. You're a special woman, Juliet, but I can't… I suppose occasional lapses like last night will happen.'

Juliet stared back at him. He could see tears welling in her eyes. 'Lapses?'

'I'm sorry, you know what I mean.'

'If all of this is true, then you had no right to ask me back here last night.'

'I asked you here for dinner.'

SUSANNE HAMPTON   231

'Then why didn't you leave it downstairs?' she demanded. 'Why did you show me the master bedroom?'

'I need to get dressed. There's no point discussing this further. We made a mistake last night. We shouldn't have overstepped the line. We work together and we should not have slept together. It won't happen again. I'll make sure of that.'

'You'll make sure of that?' she repeated solemnly. 'I'll make sure of it.'

'Juliet, I didn't mean to hurt you; you have to believe me.'

'I don't have to believe anything.' She climbed from the bed and began to gather her clothes. Angrily she pushed past him to the bathroom. She slammed the door shut and reappeared a few minutes later, dressed.

'There's just one more thing,' he said, determined to distance himself from Juliet and her tiny daughter. He knew it would sound heartless but it would ensure she stopped trying to help him.

'What?' she demanded.

'Would you mind telling Bea that the delivery she's expecting won't be arriving? The Christmas tree farm can't deliver. I'm truly sorry.'

CHAPTER THIRTEEN

JULIET ARRIVED HOME to see there were no missed calls from Charlie. He hadn't so much as sent her a text, let alone called to apologise or try to make it up to her. Her face was damp with tears she had shed but most of them had rolled down her cheeks on the short and painful drive home just before dawn. The road was dark and she felt more alone than she had ever done before.

It was her worst nightmare. A one-night stand with a man with whom she had thought she might possibly fall in love. If she wasn't already a little. With a heart heavier than she had dreamed possible, Juliet had run out of his home when he'd told her about the tree. She'd known she had to leave. Without saying another word.

She'd had to turn her back on Charlie Warren just the way he had turned his back on her.

But before he'd seen the tears she had promised herself all those years ago that she would never shed for a man.

She had pulled into her driveway and crept into the house before the sun came up and slipped into bed beside Bea, feeling stupid and filled with regret. She hoped her daughter would never make the same mistakes she had, twice. She wanted so much more for Bea. She wanted her to feel real love, the kind that lasted for ever with the bells and whistles and everything a man could give and that neither had given to Juliet.

She could hear her father snoring in the other room and knew her mother would be wearing the earplugs that had saved their marriage. Her father's snoring at times was like a long freight train rattling down the tracks, and, without the earplugs, she knew her mother would have gone mad from the sleep deprivation or divorced him. But she had found the solution in a pharmacy, popped them in her ears and had her happily ever after. For Juliet there was nothing in a pharmacy, no prescription or over-the-counter solution to her woes. She simply chose the wrong man and that was a problem that couldn't be cured.

In her lifetime Juliet had only chosen two men and both were wrong for her. And both were nothing more than one-night stands.

There would be no happily ever after.

She was, in her mind, the poster girl for stupid decisions with her one hundred per cent failure rate.

Bea had left the bed while Juliet lay with her eyes closed. Now she could hear her daughter giggling over the sound of the television in the other room. She could also smell fruit toast that she knew her mother or father had prepared for their granddaughter.

While her irresponsible mother slept in after a drive of shame home.

They had been careful, so at least she had no fear of another pregnancy. No, this time she had only gained a broken heart and damaged pride. Not to mention shattered dreams that what she had shared with Charlie in his four-poster bed would amount to more than a night. Climbing from the bed, she headed for the bathroom. She needed to soak in the tub and try to wash the man out of her heart.

Only this time, she thought it would take longer and hurt more. Because this time she had believed in her heart it was real.

* * *

It was the weekend, and Juliet was not required at the hospital but she wanted to be there to see Georgina and Leo and also their babies. In general her role ended after the delivery, but the outcome of the Abbiatis' procedure was not what she had clearly hoped for and she wanted to check in with them. Despite what Charlie had said post-operatively, and what she knew to be true, she still felt responsible for the babies' pre-term arrival. It wasn't logical, it was heartfelt, and that was linked very closely to the outcome of becoming involved with Charlie.

Spending the night in his bed was illogical and…heartbreaking.

She left Bea playing cards on the floor with her grandfather. Snap was their game of choice. The house was lovely and warm and Juliet's mother was going to roast a chicken for lunch, then they thought they would all rug up in their winter best and head out for a walk through the town. Juliet wished she were in the mood to join them but decided to hide behind her work rather than pull them all down with her melancholy mood.

After parking in the hospital car park she made her way into the hospital. The chilly breeze seemed even colder that morning.

Juliet caught sight of Ella as she walked into Maternity. Worried that the midwife would sense immediately that she was upset, Juliet quickly realised that she had to avoid her. Ella had mentioned a few times how she was growing accustomed to Juliet's sunny personality and that day Juliet knew she was anything but sunny. With her head down, she waved and rushed past Ella, hoping she would assume she was in a hurry and not think anything of it. But she wasn't that lucky.

'Juliet,' Ella called to her. 'Do you know where I might find Charlie?'

Juliet shrugged her shoulders. She didn't want to be drawn into talking. She feared she might tell Ella that she hoped Charlie was rotting somewhere in hell. Or worse, burst into tears and confess how much she still felt for the man who had behaved so poorly. So she kept walking, offering Ella nothing. In Juliet's mind, it was best if she was the only person who knew about her foolish behaviour. No one else needed to know that she had actually believed, when he'd pressed his hard body against hers, that a man like Charlie wanted more than a fling.

With a deep breath to steady her emotions, she knocked on Georgina's door. There was another hurdle to face that day. Georgina and Leo and their questions about what went wrong.

'Come in,' came Leo's voice.

Juliet stepped into the room that was filled with flowers and family members. She suddenly realised she also had to face their family.

'Mum, Dad,' Leo began, then turned to the other set of parents and repeated himself. 'Mum, Dad, this is Dr Juliet Turner, the *in-utero* surgeon from Australia.'

Juliet attempted a smile. She was genuinely happy to finally meet Georgina and Leo's parents but it would have been a nicer meeting if it had occurred the previous day. Before the surgery had brought about the preterm delivery of the four babies...and before she had stupidly slept with Charlie and hated herself.

Moving closer to Georgina, she did not attempt to shake four sets of hands. The closest were folded, the next clasped, one set leaning on the window ledge and the final hands were arranging flowers. It was a little overwhelming and she suspected they were all making judgement calls on the laser surgery that had brought about the early arrival of the quads. And they had every right. While she'd known it was risky, she had forged ahead and in their eyes that was probably not the right decision.

'So you're the Australian doctor who performed Georgina's surgery?' one of the two older men said.

Juliet nodded and lifted her chin. The outcome was not perfect but Juliet still believed she had made the correct decision. The only correct decision she had made that day.

'Yes, I am. And I stand by my advice to operate. Despite the outcome, I believed then, and still believe now, that it was the best option, however—'

'Then we all owe you a huge debt of gratitude for saving our grandchildren.'

Juliet was taken aback. She'd thought both sets of parents, along with Georgina and Leo, would have been upset with her. Not grateful.

'Please take a seat. You must be exhausted after the day you had yesterday,' the taller of the two women said. 'We heard you stayed back to check on the babies. Have you seen them today? They're so tiny but the neonatologist is very hopeful they'll all pull through. They're tiny little Italian fighters.'

'You should have called Rupert Rocky instead!' Georgina's father suggested with a grin. 'It's not too late to change his name.'

'Rocky as in Rocky Balboa?' Leo asked, looking more than a little embarrassed.

'The greatest Italian fighter ever!' his father-in-law replied happily.

'Dad,' Georgina cut in, 'Rocky is a fictional character in a movie.'

'I know,' the older man replied. 'But Rupert's a fighter and the other three are just as strong. I know in my heart our grandchildren will pull through. And that's thanks to you, Dr Turner.'

'I'm not sure where this is all coming from,' Juliet admitted.

'Charlie was in early this morning to see me and check my stitches,' Georgina continued. 'He told me that, even though he was against the laser surgery, and despite it not going to plan yesterday, it saved Rupert's life because it brought on my labour early and he was born just before his heart stopped. A day longer and he would not have survived. You saved our baby's life, Dr Turner.'

'Charlie, is everything all right with Juliet?' Ella asked as she caught up with Charlie scrubbing in before visiting with the quads.

'Why? What makes you ask that?' His

tone was defensive. He didn't want to be questioned by the midwife. They had been friends for a long time but he didn't want to feel forced to justify his behaviour to anyone. There was no other choice but to push Juliet away. He had to be cruel to be kind. While he regretted hurting Juliet, he knew if he led her on he would hurt her more. It would just take her longer to feel the hurt. She was looking for a happily ever after and he was not that man. He had a debt to pay. And it wouldn't allow him to love someone. Particularly the way he knew he wanted to love Juliet. With every fibre of his being.

But he wouldn't.

'She rushed past me this morning, and snubbed me. Well, almost, I mean she waved at me but it wasn't like her. And I asked about you and she just shrugged her shoulders. She and Bea are always so lovely and she seemed upset today.'

'Perhaps she's drained after yesterday,' he suggested to deflect from the real reason.

'No, she's a pro,' Ella responded. 'She wouldn't react that way.'

'Just leave it alone.'

'You know, Juliet would be perfect for you, Charlie. I know you may not have thought about her that way, but she's beautiful, sweet and intelligent. You're both single. I think she could be *the one*, Charlie.'

'I like it on my own. It's been that way for a long time. I had *the one*, and I lost her. I don't need to hurt another woman.' It was true that it had been a long time but it was a lie that he liked being alone. It was a penance he made himself pay for the accident.

'It's been over two years since the accident—that's long enough for someone as young as you to mourn. Your wife wouldn't want you to go on punishing yourself.'

'I guess we'll never know what she wanted, because I killed her.'

'It was an accident—a stupid accident that no one could have averted. It's lucky you lived through it.'

'I'm not so sure I'd call myself lucky. I lost Alice.'

Ella shook her head. 'It was a tragic accident that you survived. You are not the first person to lose their partner. It's awful, but it happens and people have to go on and rebuild their lives.'

'It was stupid and reckless. I've no right to a happy life when my wife died with my hands on the steering wheel. I'll never forgive myself for that.'

'Charlie, I hope you know from the way Juliet and little Bea look at you, you might just be punishing more than yourself by pushing them away.'

Juliet saw Charlie around the hospital when she popped in to check on the quads over the next couple of days but he said nothing to her. He had every opportunity to try to make amends. To apologise. But he didn't try. She felt as if the world were crashing in. A world she'd dreamed she might possibly begin to build with Charlie. She knew it was too soon to have been thinking for ever, but she had. For the first time in a very long time. They had shared his bed for one night and after she'd left, they did not even acknowledge each other.

She had no idea how he could be so cold but she made a promise to herself as she heard his office door close.

She would never trust her instincts where men were concerned.

And she would never speak to Charlie Warren again. Although she doubted she would ever stop thinking about him.

CHAPTER FOURTEEN

IT WAS EARLY Monday morning when Juliet awoke. The sky was overcast and threatening to rain down on the still-damp earth. While she knew she had so much to be grateful for, it still didn't lessen the pain in her heart. But just like the dismal weather, it too would subside in time, she reminded herself. But how much time that would take she didn't know. Sitting in bed with Bea still sound asleep beside her, she thought back over the week since they'd arrived. So much had happened. The rushed journey over was probably the least eventful.

Bea's pink cast took her attention and she remembered the sinking feeling when she saw her fall to the snow. Instinctively, sitting in the warmth of her bed, with her little girl safely beside her, she still dropped her head into her hands. That fleeting but very real fear that something had happened to her daughter had been the worst feeling in the world.

And how she felt as she thought about Charlie, she accepted, was the second to worst feeling.

Losing him, after only having him for one night, brought sadness to her every thought. She had been stupid to believe there could be more. She had fallen into bed with a man once again without thinking.

Then she shifted her shoulders and lifted her chin. It wasn't quite like that, she had to admit to herself. Charlie was not just any man. He was different. Charlie never lied to her, like Brad. He didn't scheme, like Bea's father. He had never hidden the fact he liked his life the way it was. Alone. But Juliet had thought she could change that. And his clear affection for her daughter had convinced her that he was ready to open his heart to love.

But he wasn't.

Both of them were wrong.

She wasn't sure what she would do. Extending her contract with Teddy's was yet to be negotiated so she still had the option of returning home. Or perhaps going on a river cruise with her parents, she thought wryly.

In the jumble of thoughts, she decided to get up and make some tea and let Bea sleep in a little longer. She tiptoed down the passageway into the kitchen and put on the kettle. She couldn't let herself fall to pieces. Bea deserved better. She was too young to witness her mother's heartbreak. Juliet's tears would have to wait until the middle of the night, when she could cry alone and wish for what might have been.

Looking at the clock, she realised it was later than she had thought. It was almost nine. Jet lag, she assumed, had finally taken its toll on her parents. That was for the best, she thought as she sat in her pyjamas and robe, holding the steaming cup of tea at the kitchen table. Her socked feet were inside her slippers.

She thought she heard a car, but presumed it was the neighbours or local traffic passing by. It wasn't the motorbike she wanted to hear. Biting her lip, and trying to hold back the tears threatening to spill onto her cheeks, she accepted that she would never hear Charlie's motorbike in her driveway.

A rustling and thumping suddenly began. And it seemed to get louder. Pulling back her kitchen curtains, to look out of her window into the neighbour's driveway, Juliet couldn't see anything. It was the oddest sound. Nothing she could really discern so she sat back down and sipped her tea. While some said tea solved everything, she doubted it would come close to resolving her problems.

The noise changed to heavy footsteps. And they were outside her house. She crossed the wooden floorboards to the front door expecting a deliveryman. She tugged her dressing gown up around her neck and braced herself for the inevitable gust of cold air as she opened the door.

But it wasn't a delivery man.

It was Charlie.

'What are you doing here?' Her voice was not welcoming. She was hurt and angry and disappointed and more confused than ever. And the reason for her tumultuous emotions was standing on her doorstep.

'I brought the Christmas tree I promised Bea.'

Juliet eyed him suspiciously as she looked to the side of the house where the six-foot tree was leaning against the wall. Snow was covering the deep green branches that had been tied up with rope.

'Why?'

'Because, as I said, I promised to do it. I won't let Bea down.'

But you would let me down, she thought. 'That's not what you told me,' she spat back.

'I'm heading off today with my father to collect one so you can take that one back. I don't want a tree or anything from you.'

Charlie didn't flinch. 'I know you're upset with me—'

'And does that surprise you?' she cut in angrily.

Charlie looked down at his snow-covered boots for a moment before he raised his gaze back to her. 'Not at all. I deserve your anger. I behaved terribly. And I want to make it up to you. Bringing you the tree is just the start...'

'But how did it get here?' she interrupted. She hadn't heard his motorbike and there was no delivery van visible outside.

'I brought it here.'

Juliet stepped onto the freezing cold tiles of the front porch.

'How?'

Charlie paused for a moment before he turned and looked over his shoulder. 'On the roof of the car. I tied it to the roof rack.'

'But you don't drive. You haven't driven since the accident. I don't understand.'

Charlie, momentarily and in deep thought, closed his eyes. When he opened them seconds later he spoke. 'I had to drive. They couldn't deliver the tree.'

Juliet said nothing.

'I borrowed the car from the Christmas tree farm owner.'

'How long since you've driven?'

Charlie looked into Juliet's eyes in silence for a moment. 'I haven't climbed into a car... since the accident. Not to drive or be a passenger. This is the first time in two years I've been behind the wheel. I had no choice but to drive because I couldn't let Bea down.'

'Thank you for the tree. I'll get my father to help me in with it later,' she said as she stepped back inside and began to close the door.

Without warning, Charlie's boot stopped it closing. 'There's more. We need to talk.'

Juliet shook her head. 'No, Charlie, we've said everything there is to say. I know how you feel. I know you like living alone. I get it. I don't agree but I accept that it's your choice and not mine. So let's leave it at that. But thank you very much for the tree. Bea will love it.'

'Please, Juliet. Give me five minutes. This is not just about Bea. I won't ever let you down again, if you'll let me make it up to you.'

She looked at his handsome face, his stunning eyes that were pleading with her, but she couldn't let him stay. She needed space

to heal and listening to his reasons, his justi-
fication for being so cold, would not help her
to shut him out for ever. He needed to leave
before she could not control her need to stroke
the stubble on his chin with her fingers, before she reached up to kiss his tender lips with
hers the way she had that night.

'I'm busy, Charlie.' Her voice was cold but
her heart was still warm and she wished it
were otherwise.

'It's nine in the morning and I know you
don't start until one today.' He moved his foot
free. She could shut the door but he hoped
with all of his heart she wouldn't. 'Please
don't close the door on us. Not without hearing me out.'

'Why, Charlie? We've said everything there
is to say. You want to spend your life living
in regret. Living something you can't change.
You can't bring your wife back and I don't
want to talk about it any more. I can't com-
pete with the woman you lost. I'm alive and I
wanted to be there for you but you threw me
away. I have my pride and I have my daughter. And you can have your lonely existence.'

'I never threw you away. I wanted you to
walk away before I hurt you.'

'Perhaps you should have thought about
that before you invited me to stay the night,'

she argued. 'You like being alone and I was just for one night. But that's not who I am. I want something more, something you can't offer. So just stay in your glorious house by yourself. It's how you like it.'

'It's not. But it took you coming into my life to make me realise that.'

Juliet frowned and began to shiver. The cold morning air had finally cut through her thick dressing gown and pyjamas and she felt chilled to the bone.

'Can we go inside?' he asked, aware that she was not coping in the cold.

'No,' she replied flatly. 'Everyone's sleeping and I don't want them to know about what happened between us. It's over and done and they do not need to be any the wiser that their daughter made another mistake.'

'It wasn't a mistake.'

'I disagree. I think me sleeping with you was a mammoth mistake. You were almost morose when we woke. I could see you didn't want me there with you.'

'I asked you to stay. I wanted you next to me.'

'Yes, maybe you did that night, but in your heart you knew it would be over when the sun came up.' Juliet began to shake from the bitter cold…and her breaking heart. 'I just wish you'd never invited me over in the first place. I wish I'd never stayed.'

'So you regret making love to me? Do you think falling into my bed and into my arms was the biggest mistake you could have made? Because I don't. It's just taken me time to work it out in my head. And my heart.'

Juliet was angry but she couldn't lie. She didn't regret making love to Charlie. All she regretted was allowing herself to fall in love with him. 'I don't understand your question. Why are you wanting to torture me? I haven't wanted to sleep with anyone in more than four years and then I make this huge error in judgement and believe that you're different, that perhaps you're looking for something more, but I was wrong.'

'You weren't wrong.' He pulled off his heavy jacket and gently placed it on her shoulders.

'You'll freeze,' she said, attempting to give it back as he stood in a jumper and shirt. The air was misty and damp, the ground outside covered with a fresh layer of snow.

His strong hands remained resting lightly on her shoulders as he refused to take back the jacket. 'I'm warm-blooded enough to survive while you hear me out.'

Juliet hated the fact that she couldn't argue

that fact. Charlie had been warm-blooded enough the night they'd spent together to keep her fire burning into the early hours. She also hated that while his coat was heavy it felt good to have it wrapped around her. His scent, the warmth of the lambswool lining that he had heated only moments before. It felt as if it were all she would ever need but she knew it wasn't hers to keep. Because he wasn't hers to keep.

'Just let me say a few things and then if you want me to go, I will.'

'Just go now—'

'I can't and I won't. Not without telling you how I feel. How I've felt since I first laid eyes on you.'

'When you told me off for being a bad mother.'

'I didn't say those words—'

'But you thought it,' she interrupted, trying to remind herself, as much as him, why they shouldn't be together.

'I admit, I've been judging everyone but mostly myself for as long as I can remember...'

'Since the accident?'

'Yes. I've been confused and carrying guilt with me for so long that I felt lost without it.

I was driven to punish myself since that day.'
His voice was low and sombre.

'But it wasn't your fault.'

'You and everyone in this town have said
that so many times,' he stated. 'But it was
how I saw it.'

Juliet thought she heard something more in
his words but she wasn't sure. 'How you *saw*
it? So it's not how you *see* it now?'

Charlie looked at her and shook his head.
'It's not how I want to see it any more and
being with you I know that's possible.'

'What's changed?' she asked, not daring to
hope that he wanted her. And was ready to
build a life with her. And with her daughter.
The three of them as a family.

'I know that hurting you won't bring my
wife back. Nothing can. I realised that as I've
slept alone in my bed for the last two nights
wanting you beside me. Wanting to feel your
tenderness and love again. Being near you
brought my spirit back and being with you
and making love to you made me feel more
alive than I thought possible. I won't let you
go without a fight. I know that spending the
rest of my life regretting the moment my wife
and I climbed in that car two years ago won't
change anything. I will still have a place in
my heart for the woman I loved back then, but

I don't want to lose the two special women who have come into my life now. I want to live in the present and build a future and I want to do it with you. I want you, Juliet, now and for ever if you'll have me, and I want to be the father that Bea needs. If you'll let me.'

'I never wanted to fight you on that. I just wanted to love you,' she told him with tears welling in her eyes.

'I know that, Juliet, and I'm sorry. The fight was never *with* you, the fight was *with* myself and my stupidity, my need to carry the guilt like a cross and my need to punish myself to make amends. I don't want to do that any more. In the week since we met, I have been questioning everything that's been my life, my reality for the last two years. You and Bea have made me want more. You've made me want a life that's free of remorse and sad memories. You've brought a light back that I never thought I would see again and warmth that I never thought I would feel. I don't want to live in the cold or the dark any more. I want to really live again. To have you by my side for the rest of my life.'

'What are you saying?'

'Juliet,' he said, dropping to one knee and wrapping her hand into the strength and warmth of his, 'I'm asking you to be my wife.

To love me the way you did the other night. To share your life and to bring life back into my home and make me want to sleep in our four-poster bed and make love to you every night. Will you? Will you make me the man I want to be and the man I can be if you'll allow me?'

'Yes,' she answered with tears freely flowing down her face as she fell into his arms and kissed him as if there would be no tomorrow. 'Yes, of course I'll marry you. I love you, Charlie Warren.'

'And I will love you for ever, Juliet...and spend the rest of my life decorating Christmas trees with Bea...and the rest of our children.'

* * * * *

Look out for the final instalment of the
CHRISTMAS MIRACLES
IN MATERNITY *quartet*

A ROYAL BABY FOR CHRISTMAS
by Scarlet Wilson

And, if you missed where it all started,
check out

THE NURSE'S CHRISTMAS GIFT
by Tina Beckett
THE MIDWIFE'S PREGNANCY MIRACLE
by Kate Hardy

Available now!